The
Bean
King's
Daughter

The Bean King's Daughter

JENNIFER J. STEWART

Holiday House / New York

For my children

Library of Congress Cataloging-in-Publication Data
Stewart, Jennifer J.
The bean king's daughter / Jennifer J. Stewart.—1st ed.
p. cm.
Summary: When Phoebe's extremely wealthy father dies and
leaves her in the custody of a stepmother she's never met,
Phoebe and her butler cunningly plot to get rid of Vicki,
assuming she's only interested in money.
ISBN 0-8234-1644-5
[1. Orphans—Fiction. 2. Stepmothers—Fiction.
3. Wealth—Fiction. 4. Arizona—Fiction.]
I. Title.

PZ7.S84895 Be 2002
[Fic]—dc21

2001059356

Contents

1. Blonde Inheritance

"But why? I told you I want you to come in with me." Even as I asked I knew the answer. I've lived with Henry as long as I can remember and I could read his poker face.

Just as he can read mine. "You know why, Miss Phoebe," the butler answered. "It's un—"

"—suitable, I know. And unacceptable, unallowable, unseemly . . ." Unfairly, I was running out of adjectives. I took a deep breath. "*Unfortunately,* I don't care! I *need* you in there, Henry."

Henry raised his eyebrows at me, but he's always doing that. It's his job. He bent down to whisper, "He's only a lawyer. They don't bite."

Right. I stared at him with my X-ray vision. You can go without blinking for a long time if you practice.

Henry backpedaled. "Well, some do—if the occasion calls for it—but you're his client. That makes you—"

"The boss?"

"Exactly. Now, I'll run down and get a *Tribune* to keep me company. I promise faithfully not to do the crossword puzzle without you." Awkwardly patting my shoulder, he abandoned me to my fate.

The lawyer's hair had long since abandoned him, except for some stubborn high-altitude tufts clinging to his ears. He stood up creakily and introduced himself when I walked in. Mr. Grossbeak's teeth gleamed sharp and yellow.

"We'll get started as soon as your, er, stepmother arrives," the lawyer informed me. "If you please, miss." He gestured to a seat across the conference table.

I hate waiting. It's not something I do well, but anyway I sat down. From the depths of the highly polished table my small face peered up at me like a phantom. Gold-rimmed glasses threatened to ski down my nose.

2

Waiting is boring. I got up and looked out the window.

Even in the late March drizzle, Chicago's State Street bustled: limousines and town cars the size of matchbox toys jockeying to double-park, bug-sized pedestrians with umbrellas scurrying faster than the cars. From twenty-eight floors up, it was like watching television with the mute on—and about as interesting. I sat down again.

"Coffee, miss? Oh, forgive me, perhaps pop?" Mr. Grossbeak asked.

I shook my head. Clearly the lawyer wasn't used to children.

There we had something in common. I'd spent most of my life around grown-ups—mainly my butler, Henry. He Who Is Never Unsuitable.

Mr. Grossbeak scratched notes with a fountain pen on a yellow pad. Catching my eye, he explained, "I can't waste time at the rates I charge."

"But aren't I paying for your time now, Mr. Grossbeak?"

His eyebrows lifted like Henry's, only bushier. "Yes, in a way, that's true. Though you are a minor."

"A miner?" I imagined heigh-hoing off to work behind the seven dwarfs.

"Underage. You won't come fully into your inheritance until you are much older."

"Oh." I thought for a minute. "What's my new, er, stepmother like?"

"I've never met her, but I presume she falls into the same category as your previous, er . . . I mean, I would prefer not to speculate." His mouth clamped shut.

Mr. Grossbeak's evolutionary ancestor had to have been a crocodile. I wouldn't get any more out of him, any more than I'd gotten out of Henry. When I read about orphans in books—leatherbound with color plates and raised letters you can feel on the page—they all have happy endings.

Not in real life. I understand I'm the leftover no one wants to touch, the kind you save long enough for it to get lost in the back of the refrigerator and grow fuzzy green mold. Thrown out in the end, because it isn't needed or wanted.

As an experiment, I spun my chair. Well oiled, it rotated soundlessly, but Mr. Grossbeak's frown sent my foot braking.

It wasn't fair. Albert Marchant had been eighty-one, and I had just turned twelve when he died. Suddenly I remembered laughter, a creaky wheeze ending in a gasp, when Poppy introduced me to one of his factory managers as his "biological possibility." Tears tried to leak out, and I shut my eyes tight against their wetness. You wouldn't catch me crying in front of a crocodile.

My fingers worked over my dress pleats, smoothing them over my knees. Poppy had ordered the dress for my birthday. I wore matching shoes and carried a handbag with a clasp that snapped like a small dog's jaws. The purse wasn't strictly necessary, but I keep feminine protection in it, prepared to become a woman.

Another thing I've noticed about orphans in books: None of them have periods. To excuse their authors, most of the books I read were written over sixty years ago. Life's messy bits got ignored then, according to Henry.

This is what Henry said about Poppy: "There was too much time lost between you and Mr. Albert, nearly seventy years, but you still shared a special bond."

No one would replace Poppy. To be honest, though, sometimes when I saw my father, it felt like I was getting an audience with the king. That's what *Fortune* magazine had called Albert Marchant: the Bean King. It said so all in capital letters right on the cover, where he had posed standing on a hill of navy beans with my stepmother Aimee.

That was two stepmothers ago.

No. Make that three stepmothers.

I, Phoebe Caroline LeBourget Marchant, am the Bean King's daughter. His only child.

The door opened. "Ms. Vicki Marchant," the secretary announced.

The Bean King's widow, last and luckiest in my long string of stepmothers, strode in. She could have walked off the inside cover of a thick romance novel, only with updated clothes, not those silly falling-off ones. She had long legs, shown off by her short red skirt. Vicki wore a matching military-styled jacket with big gold buttons. Masses of blond hair grazed her shoulders. Based on looks alone, if Vicki were auditioning for the role of evil stepmother in a fairy tale, she wouldn't get the part.

In the movies, though, she might.

She looked too young to be anybody's mother.

"Sorry I'm late," Vicki apologized. "Those reporters! And cameramen! They've been following me everywhere. Plus, I got lost and had to stop for directions. Even then, I had to guess. Where's Bert's lawyer gonna hang? I figured the tallest building around."

Mr. Grossbeak waited while Vicki settled herself. Wasting little of his hourly fee on introductions, he tented his fingers together and began. "My lifelong client, Mr. Marchant, your father," he nodded at me, "and your husband," he sniffed at Vicki, "made a habit of revising his will about as often as he married. In a nutshell, all the proceeds of his estate—the bean processing plants, his stocks, his investments, the mansion, the hotel where you've been staying—"

"He owned the hotel suite?" Vicki asked.

"He owned the hotel." Mr. Grossbeak looked down at his notes, but his train of thought appeared to have been derailed.

"Etcetera," I prompted.

"Yes, etcetera."

"He apparently had a lot of etceteras," put in Vicki. "Get on with it."

Mr. Grossbeak sent her a quelling look. "He left everything in trust to Phoebe. As for you, Ms. Marchant—"

"Vicki."

"Er . . . Ms. Vicki . . . There is a lifelong annuity—as long as you don't remarry—per the

7

prenuptial agreement of three hundred thousand dollars per year." He looked at me and explained, "What she signed so that when she and Mr. Marchant divorced—"

"Hey, who says we would have?" Vicki exclaimed.

Oh, statistics. Probability. And five ex-stepmothers before her. It was easy to peg Icky Vicki into the never-going-to-be-a-rocket-scientist-in-a-million-billion-years category.

Mr. Grossbeak closed his eyes. "My apologies, madam. What Mr. Marchant also decided was that you, madam, myself, and one other person, who prefers to remain anonymous at this point, are to be the trustees. Mr. Marchant entrusted me to take care of the financial management. He had a more, uh, personal role in mind for you, Ms. Vicki."

"Wait a sec—just how big was Bert's estate, Mr. Grossbeak?"

"In the neighborhood of three hundred sixty-five million."

My stepmother appeared stunned, as though a vet had zapped her with a tranquilizer gun. Her voice shook when she said, "Ten days ago, I knew my bank account to the penny, Mr. Grossbeak, and today, you're rounding to the nearest million. I can't even count that high." She closed her eyes, and slowly, very slowly, a smile spread across her face, almost to her ears. "But, I'll have a lot of fun trying!"

She dug into her purse. Holding a hairbrush up like a microphone, she deepened her voice. "Vicki, if someone gave you three hundred sixty-five million dollars, what would you do with it?" She wrinkled her forehead, as if thinking, then switched to a breathy voice. "I would, um, use it to promote world peace, make sure all kids can read, feed the homeless, and uh . . . save all the endangered species of the world!"

Mr. Grossbeak cut her off. "If you're quite finished?" The ice behind his tone would have caused frostbite in anyone else.

The young woman slipped the hairbrush back into her purse. She turned to me. "I mean, don't get me wrong. I'm sorry Bert's dead and all. Your father and I were just getting to be good friends. I knew he had money, but I had *no* idea. No idea at all." Then she asked the lawyer, "So, do I, like, get any more, if I take on Phoebe?"

Cautiously Mr. Grossbeak nodded. "If you share a household, all common expenses will be picked up. And an additional sum will be settled on you." He consulted his notes. "Ten million dollars. Additional funds would require approval, but any reasonable request would be met. In view of the fact that you are, er . . . I mean, were his wife, rather than his ex . . ."

I stared at the woman as she fussed with her hair. I felt dazed. Now I understood I wasn't exactly a leftover, unless it was a very big pile of beans. Certainly I'd inherited a problem.

Vicki's smile couldn't get any broader. She quit playing with her hair and swiveled back to me. "How old are you, Phoebe? Ten, eleven?"

"Didn't my father tell you? I'm twelve." So that Vicki wouldn't have to do the math, I added, "It will be nearly six years before I'm eighteen."

Vicki locked eyes with me, and just for an instant I wasn't sure if she fit the stupid step-mother stereotype I'd gotten used to—it looked like more than air space between those greedy green eyes.

Mr. Grossbeak cleared his throat. "Phoebe, your father wished for you to give this relation-ship with your stepmother a chance. Yet, he had arranged—if it doesn't work out—for you to attend boarding school in Switzerland."

Switzerland? "But—" I started to protest.

Vicki interrupted me. "Looks like we're hap-pily ever after stuck with each other, kid," she drawled. Rising, she extended her hand. "Come on, Phoebe. Let's go."

I let her hand hang there in the air. A diamond encircled by emeralds sparkled on her ring finger, showy as the rest of her. My last stepmother had worn its twin. Or maybe not? Poppy had never wasted money. He hadn't even believed in giving to charity.

"I'll prepare the paperwork for legal guardianship," Mr. Grossbeak was saying. "Let's meet in six weeks' time? In view of Phoebe's age, she'll have a lot of say in the decision."

"You mean if it doesn't work out?" Vicki stopped in her tracks. "What's not to work out? I'm her stepmother."

"Mr. Marchant did have someone else in mind. The other trustee I spoke of . . . a child can be a heavy responsibility—"

"Oh, don't worry about us. I'm sure we'll get on. We have so much in common!"

"Three hundred sixty-five million dollars," I said, before I could stop myself.

Again, Vicki surprised me. She laughed long and hard.

Poppy, how could you have done this to me?

"Miss Phoebe," Mr. Grossbeak said, "you are to call me with any problems or concerns. Here is my card. I'll check in with you next week, as your father would have wished."

That left me with no choice but to tail Vicki's

sassy chassis out the door. Where it would lead, I didn't have a clue. But then, who cared? Vicki wouldn't stick around.

None of my other stepmothers had. Why should she be any different?

As long as I didn't get sent away, I would be all right. Henry would know what to do. I held that thought close.

2. My (Evil) Stepmother

My new stepmother stuck out her hand, and Henry shook it, but his expression said he'd rather not. With Henry, trust has to be earned, and it was clear—at least to me—that Vicki hadn't passed inspection. Silently the three of us filed into the elevator. It swooshed down, taking my stomach plummeting with it. The doors opened with a soft hiss.

Five photographers ambushed us. "Vicki, Vicki! Just one shot, puleeze!"

"We'd better do it, kid. Then they'll leave us alone." Vicki bent down and hugged me around the shoulders. "A little smile," she whispered in my ear.

I bared my teeth as cameras began flashing. Then I crossed my eyes.

Porter drove the limousine much faster than usual, but it didn't matter; there were more photographers lurking in front of the mansion. Henry hurried me inside, shielding my face with his newspaper, but Vicki dawdled. Then, once inside, she just stood there with her mouth open like a fish, and Henry shut the door double-quick against the photographers.

Slowly my stepmother turned, taking in the checkered marble underfoot, the plush crimson carpeting on the stairway gracefully arching to the upper floors, and the gold-framed mirrors reflecting the light of the immense chandelier dripping prisms high over our heads. It *is* pretty impressive when you see it for the first time. Vicki was practically drooling. If she knew what had happened to the last stepmother, she wouldn't be considering moving in.

"Whoa!" Vicki exclaimed, sucking in air. "This I did not imagine. Wow! Tell me, Phoebe, do you ever slide down that banister?"

"It's not allowed," I told her. It could be a glorious ride if you remembered pillows for the crash landing, but I wasn't planning on sharing that with Vicki. Or anything else.

"So you do it when everyone's asleep?" Her eyes caught mine.

But Clara saved me, by offering to give Vicki a tour of the mansion, while one of the maids unpacked for her. Making my escape, I heard Vicki asking the plump housekeeper, "So what's it like living at Symphony Hall?"

With the sun masked by clouds, the windows in the atrium were gray and dark. A flashlight would have come in handy, but there wasn't time. Carefully I shut the door behind me to keep the heat and humidity in. The air smelled heavily of orchids, like someone had spilled French perfume. Tall palms loomed creepily, and it didn't take much imagination to picture someone hiding behind the stacks of terra-cotta pots. Maybe one of those reporters, so I checked to make sure I was alone.

Twenty-five sweaty minutes later, I had collected a dozen spiders. I peered into the jar. Two were fighting. "You can't eat each other," I lectured, "you have a job to do." Quietly I let myself out of the atrium, shivering in my dampened clothes.

Luckily the guest suite door wasn't locked. Faint noises came from the picture gallery, though, so I hurried inside. In less than thirty seconds, I twisted the lid off the jar, dumped the spiders under the pillows in the bed, and smoothed over the coverlet. Perfect. Spiders had worked their leggy magic on stepmothers number two and number four. Why mess with success?

In the closet Vicki's clothes took up surprisingly little space, not like my previous stepmothers. Altogether, they consisted of four blouses, a few T-shirts, a Bulls' sweatshirt, a raincoat, and two pairs of jeans all looking lonely on hangers. The jacket from the fire-engine red suit she'd been wearing hung at the end of the rod, keeping its distance from the more everyday items. Where were the rest of the glitzy clothes? This couldn't be Vicki's entire wardrobe. I'd have to come back to search her drawers.

I tracked down Henry in the kitchen. He turned to me and arched an eyebrow. "So? What was your father thinking?"

"It's kind of obvious he wasn't," I said. "Would you call Mr. Grossbeak now? Please?"

"Miss Phoebe, she hasn't been here twenty-four hours yet. I don't think he'd see it as a fair trial, do you? You remember what your father wanted."

*   *   *

It had been the last time I'd seen Poppy. We had been playing checkers, Henry standing like a penguin behind my father. I had my fingers poised over a checker. Henry shook his head. I moved my hand, selecting another, and Henry nodded.

"Henry," my father had said, "you are not to help Phoebe. With age comes a certain amount of wisdom. I may not have eyes in the back of my head, but I know what you're doing." His hand shaking slightly, Poppy nudged his own piece forward.

I attacked, jumping two of his checkers, losing three of my own in the process. But in the end, Poppy had had to surrender.

"Ho for you, girl! I didn't see that coming. You should be ashamed, taking advantage of an old man like that." Poppy chuckled. "Now, Henry, sit down. I have something to tell the two of you, and I can't with you towering over us. No, sit, sit! Don't stand on ceremony. And you come here, Phoebe." My father patted a place beside him and I snuggled in close, careful not to jar his old bones. I breathed in his smoky, spicy smell, a combination of the cigars he couldn't give up overlaid with bay rum aftershave.

Poppy waited until Henry had seated himself gingerly on the chair's edge. "Now, hear me out.

Fifteen years ago, I married Phoebe's mother. And she was the best thing that ever happened . . ." He stopped, unable to continue.

I put my hand in his. "Until I came along."

Poppy smiled. "Until you came along, scalawag. When your mother died, I couldn't have survived without you. But I won't outlive you, Phoebe—that's the truth, and I do need to think of your future. I don't want to leave you alone."

"You're not going to!" I protested.

Henry spoke up. "Mr. Marchant, I'll always care for Miss Phoebe, no matter what."

"I appreciate that, Henry, but Phoebe's at that delicate age. She needs a woman to talk to."

Then Poppy added, "So I've decided to remarry."

Again? "Oh, no, Poppy!"

"Oh, yes, little one. And, Phoebe? This time, give her a chance. You, too, Henry. This one's different."

How could I possibly give Vicki a chance, when right this instant she was wandering around the house like she'd won the lottery? I had to be firm. "Henry, Poppy knew more about beans than romance. I want you to get rid of her. Call Mr. Grossbeak. Now."

"No, miss. We must abide by your father's wishes."

When he calls me "miss," it usually means he thinks I'm in the wrong. "But, Henry, Mr. Grossbeak said if Vicki stayed for six weeks, she'd get ten million dollars."

That ruffled him. "No, that can't be right. Ten million for six weeks?"

"Well, it's supposed to be until I'm eighteen, but Mr. Grossbeak will give it to her after six weeks. And guardianship of me!"

Henry sighed. "We may not like the situation, but it's too soon, Miss Phoebe."

He had a point. Vicki wouldn't give up that easily. "Yes, and you know what, Henry? Whatever happens, she'll pack me off to a Swiss boarding school as soon as she gets the chance. That always happens in books. Because I'm 'an inconvenience.' And at Swiss boarding schools, they make you wear scratchy wool stockings and those little hats that look like a pancake died on your head—"

"Those would be berets, Miss Phoebe—"

"Whatever! We've just got to get rid of her, Henry. She'll ruin everything! I don't even speak Swiss!"

*   *   *

Henry's idea was to kill her with icy politeness. If he'd asked me, I could have told him that takes too long.

He served dinner in the larger of the two dining rooms. He'd made sure there was a lot of silverware to choose from, but Vicki just copied me, working from the outside forks in. Even the fish knife didn't throw her. Between courses, she quizzed me.

"So, Phoebe, tell me about yourself. Where do you go to school?"

"I attend Miss Edgecombe's School for Girls. It's very exclusive."

"Of course," said Vicki. "It would have to be. And what do you study at Miss Eggbeater's— excuse me—Miss Edgecombe's?"

"I'm studying French, of course, literature, mathematical models, history of scientific discoveries, world geography, etiquette, and financial portfolios."

"Financial portfolios?" She looked surprised.

"All young ladies should be able to read the *Wall Street Journal* and discuss it intelligently."

That shut her up. While we waited for Henry to bring in dessert, it was my turn. "Where did my father meet you?"

"He placed a personal ad; I answered it. We decided we'd suit, and we got married."

I couldn't picture Poppy doing any such thing. I mean, what would the ad say: OLD, RICH, UGLY MAN SEEKS OPPOSITE? "I don't believe you."

Vicki shrugged. "Then don't."

"Didn't it bother you that—"

"That he was twoscore and eighteen years older than me? The money more than made up for that, honey. I mean, who would you rather marry, a nice eighty-one-year-old multimillionaire or a fifty-year-old one? Right. I'm sorry he's gone, though. We would have done a lot together, the three of us."

That we would have been one happy family I found harder to swallow than Vicki saying the age difference didn't matter. It had mattered to me! She'd all but admitted Poppy's money was his only attraction. Besides, she didn't look sorry. She looked like someone starving who'd just been handed the room service menu at a five-star hotel.

"It wouldn't have happened," I told her. "You wouldn't have lasted any longer than the others. Some of them tried being nice to me, too, you know, early on. Finally, my father just stopped introducing them to me. I mean, I didn't ever see them more than two, three times."

"You never know what might have happened,"

Vicki said, her eyes narrowing, "and you don't know me very well yet. Maybe I'm a completely different animal from your average stepmother."

Right. And maybe I'm a character in a book.

Then Vicki asked for a second helping of chocolate mousse. Henry made eyebrows at her, but she ignored them.

We finished up in silence. Just as long as the spiders frightened her, I didn't care how different she was.

Before bed, I headed for the kitchen again. Henry was washing out the coffeepot. I perched myself on one of the high stools and leaned my elbows on the granite counter.

"There's something I'm not getting, Henry."

"Tell me."

"The photographers? Why did they want to take pictures? Why did they even take some of you?"

"Ah. That. You see, they're hoping to catch your nouveau stepmother making a fool of herself, just as she made a fool of Mr. Albert."

"Maybe we should go away and just leave her. I want you to take me to Paris, Henry."

"Miss Phoebe, you can't run away from your problems."

"I just think I should see Paris in the spring-time."

"I think I am too old for that. Would you hand me that towel? Yes, that one. Thanks."

"No, you're not—what are you going to be, thirty-two on your next birthday? You just mean I'm too young."

"Perhaps" came his answer, but he smiled as he said it. "You know, the French eat lots of things you might not want to try, miss. Like escargots . . . do you know what those are?"

"I know what escargots are. I had them on my French vocabulary test. Ooh, would you serve them tomorrow?" I was willing to bet Vicki had never been faced with a plate of snails before. I would claim they gave me hives.

"Good night, Henry."

"Good night, miss. Sleep well."

Forgive me, Poppy, but I was hoping for screams in the night.

3. Get Out of Town

Snow clogged nose and mouth. Eyes burned from the cold, yet I couldn't see anything. My lungs gasped for air. I scissored my legs, straining upward. My arms flailed out, and with my last burst of energy, I broke through the crust.

Blue sky, air to gulp down! And, then, a warm wetness on my frozen cheek. I turned and looked into the sad brown eyes of a St. Bernard with a cask on his collar and a Swiss beret on his head. My furry rescuer gave my face a damp kiss and I woke up. Sheets and blankets bunched like snowdrifts around me. I thrust them away and dashed the wetness from my eyes. It was only a nightmare. Rats. Absolutely nothing else had disturbed the peace of the night.

Double Rats.

I didn't ring for Henry to bring the breakfast tray. Zipping into my clothes, I raced outside. At the back of the property, I found Sal, the head gardener, training ivy on an elephant topiary. I waited while he climbed down the ladder. Then, hands on my hips, I demanded, "Who needs an indoor rain forest when there aren't any of those neon poison frogs to go with it? Could you get some for me?"

"Yes, miss," Sal grunted, like a character in *The Secret Garden,* one of my all-time favorite orphan books. "I don't know what you need poison frogs for," he said, "but as soon as I finish the Fantasia section, miss—hippo's looking a bit fuzzy—I'll see about chartering a plane. Or would you prefer to send Clara down the Amazon?"

I was not in the mood to be teased, but it was hard not to smile, picturing our plump housekeeper stuffing her shiny black purse with amphibians. My face went all serious. "She'd have to take her vacuum cleaner to suck 'em up. You know Clara would never touch them, even if they weren't poisonous. You'd better go, Sal."

"Right after I finish the hedges, miss." This, too, was a joke, not especially funny. The hedges were never finished. Once Sal finished the front, the back needed pruning, then the sides, and so forth.

I was insisting when suddenly I heard a series of rapid clicks. Sal and I glanced up, just in time to see a dark-haired man with a camera disappearing behind the hedge.

"Who was that?" I asked.

Sal said, "Let's continue this conversation indoors, miss. I need to talk to Mr. Henry." He put down the clippers and headed for the main house. I broke into a little run to keep up.

"You won't say anything to Henry about the frogs, will you?"

"It will be our secret, miss. Was there a particular color you had in mind?"

Back in my bedroom suite, sitting at my desk, I crossed "poison frogs" off my list. Now it read:

> ~~poison frogs~~
> bald?
> snails to eat, other grossities
> haunted house of horror

I thought hard and added "*really* bad stink."

However, I didn't see Vicki until lunchtime, when she wandered into the kitchen just as Henry and I were sitting down to soup and grilled cheese sandwiches.

"Want some?" I asked. I was trying to put her off her guard.

I think Henry felt the same way, because he added, "It's tomato soup. Out of a can, but even so, quite delicious. I was going to bring yours on a tray."

"What, no filet mignon?" Vicki mocked.

"I don't like it," I said. Or you, but kept that to myself.

"Just kidding, Phoebe. No, I feel like a pizza," Vicki announced. "A big one, with everything on it. Henry, where do you hide the phone book?"

Waving off the butler's offer to call, Vicki scooped it up and left. Henry helped me with my French vocabulary, then got thoroughly confused by my math assignment. It was a good lunch.

When the doorbell rang, Vicki beat Henry to the door. She took the box from the deliveryman.

"Thanks. He'll take care of the bill for you." Vicki jerked a thumb in Henry's direction. "And give him a nice tip, won't you, Henry?"

Henry invited the deliveryman into the kitchen. He examined the bill, raised his eyebrows, and looked again.

I peeked. "That's a lot of pizza."

"There must be a mistake," said Henry.

"No mistake, sir," the deliveryman said. "Lady ordered twelve pies, but just one to come here. You are going to pay, aren't you?"

Henry got a pain on his face, but he wrote out a check. After ushering the pizza guy out, he turned to me. "I need to talk to your stepmother."

"She's not *my* anything. Are you going to call Mr. Grossbeak now?" I trailed Henry hopefully as he marched upstairs and knocked on Vicki's door.

"Who is it?" came Vicki's voice.

"May I have a word with you, madam? Please," Henry added.

"I'm kind of busy right now. Can you come back later?" floated back Vicki's reply.

"It's about the pizza bill. A dozen pies with 'the works!' You evidently had pizza sent to some of your friends?"

Vicki opened the door. A slice of pizza dangled from her right hand. "I'm sorry, should I have used a coupon?"

"Maybe you should have invited them to dine with you?"

"Oh, I didn't want to put you out, Henry. Such short notice. Oh, and Henry, skip dinner for me. This pizza will last me. Do you want a slice, honey?"

I shook my head. I had to walk fast to keep up with Henry as he stalked off.

"What are you going to do with all those snails, Henry?" Obviously, my question didn't compute. "You know, the ones you were going to serve Vicki for dinner? Could I have them?" *They* would create a really splendiferous stink given a day or two.

I was brushing my teeth when a photographer tried to snap a picture of me through the bathroom window. I screamed. Vicki ran in, took one look at the toothpaste foaming around my mouth, and screamed several decibels higher.

Henry ran in and Vicki clutched his lapels. "She's rabid! You have to do something!"

I screamed even louder. By the time it was all sorted out, the photographer had slunk away.

Next morning, Henry delivered his opinion with the hot chocolate. "Madam, it's simple. If you leave, you'll take all the photographers and nosy reporters with you. Miss Phoebe and the staff will be left in peace. We're virtual prisoners here; with you gone, they'll let us out. It would be better for Miss Phoebe."

"Jail" was the red parlor, a room I hadn't been welcomed in as a child with sticky fingers. From where I sat, I looked out the window towards Lake Michigan's wind-tossed whitecaps.

Across from me, my stepmother reclined on a chaise longue, preferring the view of Monet's *Waterlilies* hung above the fireplace. "I wonder how much that's worth?" she said. She looked relaxed and well rested.

It was totally annoying.

Vicki sipped from her teacup, pinkie cocked just so. "Do they leave the prince of England alone? You forget, they can't take any more pictures of Bert with some Vegas sweetsie on his arm: LOOK WHO HE'S MARRYING NOW! No, Henry, Phoebe's tabloid news as much as I am. She's about the richest kid in America, right? And how many kids do you know who control half the world's bean supply?"

"Well, madam," Henry asked, "do you have a better suggestion? The *National Enquirer* has accosted Clara. And when Porter tried to drive Phoebe to school, three photographers popped up like jack-in-the-boxes to take her picture!"

"I'll survive that," I put in. Swiss boarding school loomed large, dank, and cold in my imagination. "Miss Edgecombe said I could work at home until the reporters go away."

"Quiet, the two of you," Vicki said. "I'm trying to think."

"God forbid," I thought I heard Henry mutter. I stared at him curiously. No, it must have been my imagination.

Vicki knitted her eyebrows together in concentration. "Henry, do sit down," she said. "You're glowering at me. I can feel it."

Henry continued to stand.

Vicki jumped to her feet and snapped her fingers. "I've got it!" She vaulted over the bow-legged coffee table and grabbed my hand. In the clipped tones of a '30s Chicago gangster, she said, "We'll blow this joint, doll face."

"What?" Henry and I asked.

"There are places no one will follow, if we cover our tracks."

"I must register my objections," Henry said. "I'm not sure this would have met with Mr. Albert's approval."

Vicki dismissed the butler's concerns with a wave. "Well, I met with Mr. Albert's approval, so what I say goes. Besides, we won't be gone long. Trust me. It'll work."

We had no reason to trust her, but we agreed to get out of town.

It was early the next morning and even though the mansion was rumored to be haunted, my stepmother looked well rested. Sitting on a suitcase in the entrance hall, I couldn't quite stifle a yawn, but jumped up when Henry made a grand entrance coming down the stairs.

"This is not going to work." Henry was emphatic.

"Henry, were you born under a sopping wet blanket, or what?" Vicki asked. "Of course it's going to work. These are not rocket scientists we're trying to fool. They're reporters. What they see is what they think."

"You've got to stop tugging on the wig, Henry," I told him. "You're making it lopsided. You really make a good-looking Vicki."

Luckily Henry had a thin build. With a curly wig on his head, a scarf to hold it in place, Vicki's trench coat belted over his own navy trousers, and her rhinestone-studded sunglasses perched on his nose, he could indeed pass for Vicki, in a dim light. If you didn't get too close.

"I don't think so," said Henry.

I ignored this. "Good thing Vicki's tall," I said.

"Couldn't Porter be the one?" Henry asked for about the zillionth time. "Porter likes dressing up. Porter does community theater in his off hours, Porter—"

"—has to drive away in the limo really fast, so that some of the reporters, maybe all of them, chase him, instead of us. Stop whining."

"I am *not whi*—"

"Wait a sec," I broke in. "Something's missing . . ." I stepped back. "Oh, I know!" I ran up the stairs and returned with a tube of lipstick. I handed it to Vicki.

"Pucker up, mister," Vicki said. "You've got to look enough like me, as if you were trying to slip out incognita—"

"In-cog-what-a?" I asked.

"Incognita, like in disguise? Henry's got to look enough like me that the photographers follow him—me—you follow?"

As a bonus, Henry couldn't argue while Vicki made his lips redder and fuller.

"Well?" Vicki asked me, "what do you think now?"

I eyed Henry critically. "Better stick out your chest some more, Henry. You might need more stuffing."

"And you need to practice my walk again," Vicki added.

Henry refused on general principles.

"Stop! What are we going to do about the shoes?" I pointed. Henry's black shoes stuck out like clown feet.

"We're not going to do anything about the shoes," Henry said.

He was right. Even though Vicki sported size 10s ("big feet go with the height, darlin' "), like Cinderella's uglier stepsister, Henry couldn't cram his long toes into Vicki's shoes. I had to hope no one checked out his feet.

"No one, but no one, looks at my feet when I come into a room," Vicki assured us. "Not since I was thirteen."

Despite Henry's doubts, the plan worked. Porter sped away with Henry dressed as Vicki in the limo, and five minutes later, Sal sped off with Vicki and me to O'Hare International in his truck. At first we scrunched down, but after a bit Sal pronounced it safe. For the rest of the ride, he and Vicki bored me with bromeliads and the least toxic way to combat the atrium's white fly infestation. I listened carefully, but nothing was said about spiders.

*   *   *

As arranged, Henry met us in the airline departure lounge. The three of us sat by the window with our backs to the other travelers, just in case. Henry reported on his adventure in a whisper.

"They took a picture of you—me?—going into the men's room?" Vicki's mouth hung open in shock. "The *men's* room?"

"It's where I normally go, you know." Henry tried, but not hard enough, to keep the smile off his face. "I did lock the door, so they weren't able to follow me. Then I changed back into my regular clothes and left. They pushed past me trying to spot, er, you."

"Can't you just see the headline?" I said.

Vicki groaned. "I just hope my aunt doesn't."

I slunk down low in my airplane seat, sandwiched between Henry and Vicki. "Everyone's staring," I complained to Henry. "The food is *bad*. And why are we sitting back here? We always sit up front."

Henry put down the airplane safety instruction card he'd been studying and addressed my concerns one by one. "We can't sit in first class. It would draw attention. This is coach-class food, and it's not that bad. Perhaps if you removed your sunglasses, Miss Phoebe. You look strange with them on. That may be why people are staring."

"Or maybe it's that Shirley Temple getup," Vicki observed.

"What's wrong with my dress?" I asked. She should talk. At least for today, though, Vicki had toned down her clothing, substituting jeans and a baggy sweater for one of her stop-traffic skirts.

With a wide gesture, Vicki said, "Look around."

On the way to the bathroom, I did. There were people in jeans, sweats, even shorts, and older couples in knits. Only one person wore a silk dress with a big lacy collar. Yours truly was more dressed up than even the crisply uniformed flight attendants doling out packets of honey-roasted peanuts.

Studying my reflection in the mirror, I ditched the sunglasses for my regular frames. I undid the braids and riffled out the hair. Now it stood away from my face like a lion's mane. I tucked the collar into my dress. It itched, but not too bad.

"Better," approved my stepmother, when I slipped back into my seat. "It's more retro-looking now, don't you think?"

"I suppose." I shrugged, unwilling to give her credit. To shut her out, I opened an orphan book.

Henry refused to be drawn into conversation. But he whispered to me, when Vicki took her turn in the lavatory, "If you can put up with this nonsense, Miss Phoebe, then so can I. At the end of six weeks, Mr. Grossbeak hands over ten million dollars—you know she's not leaving without the money—and then, guess what? Abracadabra! Vicki with two *i*'s will disappear, and we'll never have to see her again."

This was quite a long speech coming from Henry. I suspected it might not be that simple. Maybe Vicki would hold out for twenty million dollars, for instance.

"And what about the anonymous trustee, Henry? Whoever replaces Vicki could be a lot worse."

Henry snorted. "Anyone would be better than Vicki," he said. "I wouldn't worry about it."

When Vicki returned, she looked at Henry and smiled sweetly. "If I were you, I'd scrub that lipstick off before we land."

4. Heat's on in the Desert

"A place no one will follow." Vicki got that right.

I stared out the rental car window at dusty gray green mountains stretching off in the distance. Not straight out of "America, the Beautiful," far from any purple mountains' majesties, their zigzaggedy edges made a cutout backdrop against the dazzling blue sky. On both sides of the road, occasional pale green cactus punctuated scrubby no-color bushes. The tallest ones had multiple arms. If any plant could be first cousin to an octopus, these were; they were truly weird looking.

"Saguaros," Vicki said, taking one hand off the wheel to point. "They don't live anyplace else in the world."

"*Carnegiea gigantea.*" Henry one-upped her. "They can live more than three hundred years."

Over two hundred years older than Poppy. Why should a stupid cactus live longer?

In the front seat Vicki and Henry were still sparring. "What are you, some kind of talking encyclopedia?" Vicki asked. But at least for now, her voice had lost its sting.

Henry didn't bother answering. Pretty soon I saw he'd gone to sleep, lulled by the endless straight road ahead.

"So, where are the trees hiding?" I finally asked.

"They're here," said Vicki. "Not as big as you're used to, and some of them even have green bark. Plus, they have small leaves. Back East, trees hide everything, like big green monsters. In the West, trees don't cover up the scenery."

I glanced curiously at the mountains again. Without its tall buildings and trees, Chicago would stretch out flat and wide in all directions. Here the landscape stood undressed. I pictured myself on a mountaintop, the one that looked like a finger. If I turned around slowly, what would I see? It might be possible to like mountains. Mysteriously massive, they grow on you. Unlike stepmothers.

Although, I corrected myself, a certain step-mother was growing on me like a parasite.

But so far, Vicki's plan was working. When the three of us stepped outside the airport into the blinding Arizona sun, no camera shutters clicked in our faces. Then once we'd escaped the city, we'd left all traffic behind. I hadn't seen a single car in the last half hour.

"How much farther?" Hot and tired, I had stopped trying to understand the strange landscape.

Her eyes hidden behind sunglasses, Vicki checked me out via the rearview mirror. "Not far. If I remember right, two more windmills and we'll be there."

After one windmill, I saw a girl in cutoff jeans and T-shirt, walking her dog—the ugliest dog I'd ever seen in my life. I rubbed my eyes. Wait, it wasn't a dog.

"Vicki? There's a girl walking her sheep or goat or something."

Vicki laughed. "Yeah, I guess it is getting on county fair time. She's practicing getting the animal used to walking by her side, ready to be in front of the judges."

"Judges?"

"Yeah, they judge all the livestock, rabbits,

cavies—those are guinea pigs, you know, not really pigs except when there's anything to eat—plus, there's cattle, goats, sheep, horses, you name it. They give out prizes. I'll take you, that's a promise."

Vicki turned right onto the next dirt road. LAZY V RANCH, a sign proclaimed truthfully, needing a coat of paint to pick out its faded letters. Probably nobody cared; the little pepper gray rabbits certainly didn't. They were the only signs of life besides the girl and her goat. Idly, I wondered if a phone call placed to Mr. Grossbeak would send him rushing to my side, like a knight of old with arthritis.

Because there had to be telephones. I could see the wires. And Henry would have packed the cell phone.

Henry woke up as we bumped along the dirt track until we reached the house. A spread-out, one-story structure, it looked as if it was made of dried mud with stones and pebbles worked into the mix. A low-slung porch shaded its windows. Chickens scattered in all directions as Vicki pulled in under the grudging shade of a tree.

The screen door banged open and a thin woman stepped out onto the porch. She had long gray hair pulled back in a ponytail. The woman shaded her eyes against the intense afternoon sun. Her eyes widened in recognition and she hustled down the steps. Vicki got a long hug. Then the woman pulled back, her hands still resting on Vicki's arms, and said, "Why, Vicki, I didn't ever expect to see you back here! I thought you'd shaken ranch dust off your boots forever."

"Oh, Auntie Ed, you knew I'd come back to visit."

Auntie Ed? "Toto, we're not in Illinois anymore," I whispered to Henry. He squeezed my hand reassuringly.

Auntie Ed was saying, "Well, it's good to have you here, whatever the reason. Now introduce me to these folks."

"This is my stepdaughter, Phoebe, and her friend Henry." Auntie Ed nodded at me and shook Henry's hand.

Strange Vicki didn't call attention to Henry's position as butler, I thought. Well, maybe there wouldn't be much to butler here.

"And this is my Aunt Edna, but we call her—"

"Auntie Ed," I finished.

"And I'm mighty pleased to meet you," Vicki's aunt said. "We haven't had a child on the ranch in years, but I'll introduce you to Maribeth Mullins first thing. She lives next door."

Remembering the strange girl, I asked, "Does she have a goat?"

"Does she have a goat? Child, Maribeth has everything! You wait and see. I'm sure you'll be friends in no time. Everyone likes Maribeth."

Why people think you'll be friends with someone just because you're the same age I don't know. I doubted Little Bo Peep and I would have anything in common. However, I caught Henry's eye and didn't protest.

Auntie Ed showed us around. "This is the room you and Vicki will share."

I had never shared a room, except with Henry that one time, so he could paint my arms and legs with calamine lotion when I had chicken pox so bad. "It will be a learning experience," I replied politely.

Vicki's aunt raised her eyebrows. "It will indeed." The bedroom held twin beds covered with colorful striped blankets. Curled up in slumber on the one nearest the door was an orange cat.

"That's Fred," Vicki's aunt indicated. "Alfred, if you want to be formal-like. He thinks that's his bed, so if you pick that one, you'll be sharing with him, too."

43

I hesitated before giving Fred a tentative stroke. The cats I knew were purebreds, used decoratively like accent pillows, combed and fussed over, but quick to scratch and bite. Fred stirred and stretched. He opened sleepy green eyes and began to purr. His left ear had a chunk ripped from it. Rough neighborhood, I guessed.

"I'd like this bed," I said.

"Done," Vicki's aunt said.

Besides beds, the room held two mismatched dressers and a closet. The window had no curtains. Seeing my puzzled look, Vicki's aunt said, "There isn't anyone close by, like in a city, so you don't need any curtains. But, if you feel strange without them, Vicki can whip some up on the sewing machine quicker than spit!"

Vicki? As in my stepmother? Auntie Ed had to be confused; sometimes that happened with old people, and it wasn't nice to call attention to it. But Vicki operating machinery? Endangering her carefully manicured nails? It did not compute. Anyway, it wouldn't have surprised me if the Lazy V was named for Vicki.

Henry had a room to himself, the actual guest room. The hired man, Tim, lived in the bunkhouse. "He could room with Tim," Vicki's aunt observed, "there's plenty of room, since I don't keep but the one man. Still and all, I think Henry will be more comfortable here, and he's right down the hall."

"I'm sure I'll be comfortable," said Henry. "I don't want to put you out in any way."

Then Auntie Ed showed us the bathroom.

Before I could stop myself, I said, "I have to share this, too?"

Auntie Ed cocked her head, as if she could hear a loose screw rattling around in my brain.

Vicki drawled, "Phoebe's used to monogrammed toilet paper, Auntie Ed, but I think she'll survive."

At dinner, an old Ball canning jar served Auntie Ed as a vase. It couldn't have been further removed from the enormous Victorian silver epergne that graced the formal dining table back in Chicago if it had tried. But it didn't try, and perhaps that was the point. No perfumed hothouse blooms for Auntie Ed; it was filled with wildflowers: oranges, yellows, blues, and intense pinks. The epergne would have overwhelmed the delicate flowers. I moved in closer, the better to appreciate their small flower faces.

"Mallow, brittlebush, lupine, penstemon," Vicki named them, touching each in turn with a lacquered fingertip. "They're so beautiful, Auntie Ed! The rains must have been good this winter to put on a show like this. The desert is so green."

Green? This dusty dried-up place? Vicki had to be kidding. I looked at Henry. He shrugged his shoulders.

Dinner turned out to be as simple as the flowers: hamburgers on buns with all the garnishes, potato salad, carrot sticks (Auntie Ed called them "rabbit food"), and canned peaches, with ice cream on the patio for dessert.

"I've never seen a sky like this," I said. It looked like someone had spread softened rainbow sherbet across it. Where the landscape looked like someone had been chintzy with the leaves and stubby trees, here no expense had been spared.

As if she'd read my mind, Auntie Ed said, "Yes, Arizona sunsets are priceless. I have to come out and watch each and every one. Don't want to miss a day. You'll see—tomorrow's will be totally different, but just as beautiful."

Tim, the hired man, joined us for an ice-cream cone. He was very tall, a good five inches on Henry, and equally thin. In the fading light he cast a long shadow and the planes on his face appeared chisel cut. He didn't say much, but dark brown eyes set alongside a weathered nose took in my silk dress and Henry's blue trousers, their creases still sharp despite the long day traveling. Tim chewed on this like bubble gum that'd lost its flavor. City folks, his expression said. Useless. Tim dignified Vicki with a hello, but that was it.

I noticed that none of them said much. Auntie Ed caught Vicki up on local gossip, but the questions she must have wanted to ask her niece, she wouldn't ask in front of Henry and me.

Suddenly, Auntie Ed turned to Vicki. "Underwear catapult!" she said, and burst out laughing. "I just remembered."

Vicki tried to be serious but failed. Smiling, she said, "Auntie Ed, you can't tell all my secrets. Phoebe and Henry don't know me too well, yet. You'll give them the wrong impression."

Auntie Ed winked at me. "I don't know about that."

"I've already formed an impression of Vicki," I said.

Vicki looked at me strangely. "Someone's taught you—was it Henry?—that if you can't say anything nice, don't say anything at all. Well, it's good advice."

I'm sure my face took on some of the sunset's hues.

Thankfully, Henry came to my rescue. "Vicki is, er, unique."

"Well, aren't we all?" said Auntie Ed.

After washing up, Auntie Ed said she was turning in. "Getting up early, you know." Henry said he would do the same. I trailed after him and whispered good night in the hallway. I couldn't stop yawning.

As I crawled between the sheets, my feet bumped against Fred's solid warmth. The cat made a lazy swipe at my toes before laying his head down again.

"Keep the light on, Phoebe—I'll be there in just a minute," Vicki called from the hallway. Then she stuck her head around the door. "Oh, and shake your shoes out before you put them on in the morning. You haven't seen any Arizona bugs yet. A scorpion could be taking a siesta in there, and you wouldn't want to rile him. We're a long way from the closest hospital. I'll hope for your sake one doesn't crawl across your pillow."

Startled, I felt the power of those green eyes. Had Vicki noticed the bug problem in her room back in Chicago? She wouldn't be so easy to spook on her own turf. Here, she had the advantage. Certainly, I'd have to redo my list. But, right now, I was too tired, and in a strange place, so I was glad to have Vicki there, and Henry just down the hall.

Oddly content, I drifted off to sleep. The sun had set two hours ago, earlier than it did in Chicago, which seemed very far away.

If any coyotes yippie-yi-yeyed in the night, I didn't hear them.

5. A Girl and Her Goats

Come morning, Auntie Ed walked me over to the Mullinses' ranch. Already warm, the cloudless sky promised it would get a lot hotter. Auntie Ed pointed out birds and cactus along the way, some of the former nesting among the stickers. "Between you and me, Phoebe," she confided, "I don't know how they stand it, but it's good protection from predators."

"Predators?" What could be lying in wait for me in this lonely place?

"Coyotes, snakes, hawks, bobcats—those are the main ones," Auntie Ed explained, ticking them off on weather-beaten fingers.

"Are they a threat to people?" I asked.

"Not usually, why?"

I kicked a stone. "Something Vicki said."

"You know, that niece of mine is prone to exaggeration. Prone to a lot of things actually." But Auntie Ed said it with a smile. "Why are you walking that way?"

"What way?"

"Like a crab. Scuttling sideways every now and then."

I stopped. "Vicki said saguaros could fall on you after it rains. She said if the weight didn't get me, I'd bleed to death from all the little punctures."

Auntie Ed snorted.

I had a sudden suspicion. "It hasn't rained in a while, has it?"

"Nope."

"I don't have to watch out for saguaros falling down, do I?"

"Nope. That Vicki."

We tramped on. "Did it surprise you when you heard she'd married my father?" I blurted out.

Auntie Ed hesitated. "Well, she explained it to me. It seems strange, but once you understand how Vicki's mind works, it makes a crazy kind of sense. She was always looking for the shortest distance between two points."

"You mean, like geometry?" I asked, confused.

"Vicki always did like multiplication best. Why?" Auntie Ed was looking at me intently.

"Oh, I was just curious." Thankfully Auntie Ed didn't pursue it. And, without having to say it directly, she had just confirmed my opinion of Vicki. You might as well tattoo dollar signs on my forehead.

Mrs. Mullins met us at the back door. The kitchen smelled of banana bread, and Mrs. Mullins cut me a thick slice, pouring coffee for Auntie Ed and herself. She shouted for Maribeth and Jessie Ann to come and meet me.

Maribeth was shorter than me by a couple inches, with brown hair plaited into two thick braids Dorothy-in-Oz style. Her blue eyes looked me over, widening as she took in my dress. It was the simplest one I had, just a little lace, but evidently far fancier than anything she owned. The girl tugged on her T-shirt self-consciously and muttered, "Hi."

"How do you do?" I replied, the all-purpose phrase Miss Edgecombe had drilled into me. It missed its mark with Maribeth. She just stared.

Jessie Ann looked like her big sister in miniature, right down to the constellation of freckles on her snub nose. "I'm five," the little girl announced. She wore a purple-fringed cowgirl dress over scuffed red boots. "My dress twirls! Does yours twirl?"

"I don't know. I've never tried."

Jessie Ann stared at me openmouthed. "Why not?"

Mrs. Mullins broke in to try and persuade Jessie Ann to put on something else. "I need to wash that dress. You wore it yesterday."

"And the day before," added Maribeth. "You wear it every day, Jess."

"But it's my favorite!" protested Jessie Ann.

In the end, Jessie Ann was talked into searching the closet for her second favorite, a red number with a twirly lace flounce. Auntie Ed gave me a nudge and I followed the two girls down the hall.

Maribeth shared a bedroom with her little sister. Like the one I shared with Vicki and Fred, the feline, twin beds with matching coverlets dominated the space. The resemblance ended there, because every surface—nightstands, dressers, bookshelves, even the Jessie Ann–sized table—was covered with tiny toy figures. A collection of ponies had been stabled on the little girl's dresser.

"This one's my favorite," Jessie Ann said, selecting a lavender pony with long curling hair and stroking it lovingly. "See? I can put different colored hair on them." She clipped on a length of orange tail. "You can comb them, too." She held out her treasure and a tiny brush.

Not wanting to be rude, I took them, but no way was I combing a pastel pony's tail, no matter how cute. Shyly, I volunteered, "Henry and I play this game—"

"Who's Henry?" asked Maribeth.

"The but—" I remembered I was supposed to keep things secret. "I mean, well, he's my friend. He takes care of me. Anyway, we play this game. We call it reincarnation—"

"I like carnations," Jessie Ann broke in. "I gave my teacher some green ones on St. Patrick's Day. They had died."

"They *were* dyed," said her sister. "Not flowers, Jess. Reincarnation."

"Like, what would something be in its next life?" I added. "Or what it was in its past one?"

"Oh," said Jessie Ann. She started combing another horse's tail.

"So, I was thinking—you know, if Barbie were ever reincarnated, she'd come back as a toy pony. Trotting around on her high hooves."

Maribeth giggled. "Phoebe, you're kind of weird."

Weird? "I'm not the one who walks goats on a leash. Now that's what I call strange."

For her part, Maribeth collected blown glass figures, which Jessie Ann was forbidden to touch: tiny little elephants, turtles, dolphins, and more. The girl could have overflowed several arks.

I picked up a miniature green dragon. "I have an art glass collection, too. I get a new piece every year at Christmas from—" I was going to say "my father," but stopped. After all, I wouldn't be getting any new pieces, would I? I set the dragon down.

Maribeth eyed me curiously. Then she said, "Now you have to come outside and meet the real critters." She hesitated. "That is, if it's okay with your aunt . . ."

"What do you mean? Anyway, she's not my aunt."

"Well, you might get your dress dirty."

I shrugged. "Henry can buy me a new one."

Auntie Ed hadn't lied when she said Maribeth had everything. I met the hens and their chicks, plus their proud papa rooster. Maribeth thrust a battered coffee can my way.

"What's this for?" I asked.

"Just take some corn out and scatter it. Where are you from, anyway?"

Chicago was as foreign to Maribeth as chickens were to me. I took a handful of corn—the un-popped kind—and threw it on the ground. Forgetting their manners, the chickens rushed about, pecking madly. I jumped back in fright, and Maribeth laughed. Next the girl showed me the guinea pigs—a lot of plump fur balls—which whistled shrilly when they spotted Maribeth (and wouldn't shut up until they each got a carrot chunk). She plunked one in my lap and it peed on me. After that, she introduced me to a fat pony named Lily. The pony thrust her soft brown velvet nose into my dress, looking for food. When she didn't find any, she licked the dress, leaving my front sloppy and wet.

Maribeth pushed the pony's nose away. "Yuck, Lily, is that any way to treat a guest?" Maribeth got out more carrots and showed me how to feed the unrepentant pony, with my palm flattened so that my fingers wouldn't be mistaken for food. She explained, "Lily wouldn't bite you on purpose—not like some ponies—but she could get mixed up. Do you want to ride her?"

For a small horse, she looked awfully big. "Oh, I don't know, Maribeth . . ."

"It's not hard, and I'll lead you around," the girl persisted.

"Well—all right. I guess. If you think it's safe."

"Safer than riding Jessie Ann's rocking horse, cross my heart. I'll just tack her up." Maribeth scooted into the corral and put a halter on Lily. She tied her to the rail fence, then ran back into the horse barn. She returned, hefting a saddle and striped blanket. In no time, she had it buckled around Lily.

"Ready?"

"What do I do?"

"Come over here, no, not that side. This one. You always do stuff on a horse's left side."

"Why's that?"

"'Cause they're used to it. They just don't like surprises. Put your left foot up here, hold with your hands here, and pull yourself up. That's it!"

I squirmed up straight and clutched the thing that stuck out like a doorknob on the front of the saddle.

"You look grand up there, Phoebe. How do you feel?"

"A lot taller."

Maribeth laughed. She adjusted the stirrups, then opened the gate. I tried to make my rear end go up and down with the pony's, but soon gave up and just leaned back and listened to Maribeth pointing out desert features. People seemed to want to do that: to show off the desert as though they were proud of every teensy tiny sticker. If Maribeth ever came to Chicago, I'd have to show her a *real* tree.

I stopped myself. If Maribeth became my friend—if I even wanted a friend here—it would be temporary like Vicki. The only thing forever was Poppy gone.

The other girl broke into my thoughts. "Are you ready to go back, Phoebe?"

"I'm okay. Maybe you're getting tired of leading me."

"Oh, that's no problem," Maribeth assured me, "only, I know it's more fun when you tell the horse what to do."

"Like this?" I made my voice low and stern. "Stop, Lily." The pony continued plodding. "She's not stopping. Okay, *go* then." I looked behind her. "She's going now. Good fertilizer, I expect. Now go left, Lily. No, she's going right. She doesn't appear to know her right hoof from her left. Now she's eating weeds—"

Maribeth was laughing so hard she was holding her stomach with both hands. "Oh, stop, Phoebe. It hurts! You tell her with your hands, your knees, and your heels—not your mouth—"

"I knew that," I said.

"You did not."

"Sshh . . . don't let Lily know. She thinks I'm the boss."

After brushing down Lily and checking her hooves for stones, Maribeth showed me a mama goat with two babies. One jumped up to nibble on Maribeth's hair ribbon. She pushed him down and he settled for my shoelace instead. I patted him gingerly. His coarse gray fur lay flat against his round body.

"That one's Tarzan and this one's Jane, of course."

"What's the mother goat's name?" I asked.

"Mrs. Tootles. Hey, if you let him do that to your shoe, you'll need to buy new laces. Give him this instead." She handed me a fistful of hay.

Tarzan wasn't to be distracted from the tasty double bowknot. "It's okay. I don't mind."

"You got to remember with goats. He acts just like a kid and that's exactly what he is. Baby goats are kids, get it?"

I got it. I'd never had a kid sister or brother before, let alone a goat. I wondered what it would be like. And, sitting at the table over lunch with Mrs. Mullins and her daughters, I wondered what a real family would be like.

On those rare occasions when I'd joined Poppy for dinner, it had been a formal affair, with more silverware than words spread over frosty white linen and little molded pats of icy butter that refused to melt. Not comfortable, like when Henry and I ate in the kitchen and played games together after I finished my homework. But this felt all right, even with Maribeth and Jessie Ann sniping at each other every now and then. Mrs. Mullins's grilled cheese sandwiches went down just fine.

When I got back to the Lazy V, Henry was puttering in the vegetable garden, gathering lettuce for a salad. He dropped a bright green caterpillar into my palm. Its legs tickled.

"Interesting creatures they've got here," he said.

"And dangerous, too," I added. "Vicki said to watch out for scorpions. Only I don't know what they look like."

"We have to watch out for Vicki more, I think." Henry plucked a cherry tomato. "Open your mouth."

The tomato tasted of sun and dust and was absolutely wonderful. "Mmm . . . do you suppose Sal would grow these in the atrium?"

"He might."

"Where should I put the caterpillar? I don't have to squish it, do I?"

Henry pointed. "Auntie Ed said that corner over there has the sacrificial plants. She's got the bunnies trained. She planted marigolds all around the other plants; something about the smell discourages them."

I searched, puzzled. "But I don't see any marigolds, Henry."

"Well, according to Auntie Ed, they all got eaten."

I found my stepmother lounging on her bed, rubbing Fred's traitorous tummy. He was drooling in ecstasy. I recognized the well-worn cover of the book she was reading, *Rebecca of Sunnybrook Farm*.

"Hey, that's my book!"

Vicki arched an eyebrow. "Sharing is loving, Phoebe—don't you know that?"

"Very funny. You sound just like that big purple dinosaur Jessie Ann watches. Besides, you didn't ask!"

"I'm sorry, your highness. You weren't around to ask." Vicki slipped a bookmark into place and swung her legs over the side of the bed. "I'm glad you're here, Phoebe. Take a good look around."

So? The room looked the same as when we'd arrived, except the floor was littered with discarded clothing.

Vicki continued, "If a space alien landed on this very spot, she'd think it was the Planet of the Dirty Clothes."

I looked at her quizzically.

"There's no maid here, darlin'."

A bulb lit up in my head. "Maybe Auntie Ed could hire someone, but you always have to check references, that's what Henry says. I'm sure Henry would do the interviewing, if Auntie Ed doesn't want to do it. He's experienced."

"Phoebe, Auntie Ed is not about to hire a maid to pick up after you."

"You want me to pick up my own socks?"

"Bright girl!" said Vicki. "I knew Miss Eggbeater's School for Girls had to teach you something. Tomorrow you'll learn even more about the real world. I signed you up for Maribeth's class at school. She'll be waiting for you out front so you can walk in together."

What? "But I don't want to go to school here!"

"Mr. Grossbeak says I'm your guardian. So because I say so—"

"Temporary guardian," I flashed back.

"Dream on, unless you'd rather go to that

fancy Swiss boarding school, Phoebe. You know, I've heard they serve grilled Swiss cheese sandwiches for lunch there every single day." With this parting shot, Vicki turned on her heel and left the room.

I admit it, the Drama Queen's exit line worried me. She wouldn't make good on her threat, would she?

No. If she tattled to Mr. Grossbeak and he was forced to call in the trustee-who-preferred-to-remain-anonymous, who would stick me *tout de suite* on the Concorde to Europe, where even Henry couldn't follow—well, I would bet it was not happening. After all, ten million dollars said Vicki wouldn't do it.

I shoved the dirty clothes under the bed. Why bother to pick them up when Henry could get Clara out here with just one phone call? It wasn't like I was going to run out of clean socks soon. And even if you towed me with a tractor, I wasn't going to school with any future farmers of America.

Well, Maribeth and her goats were all right, I guess, but there were limits. I left to find Henry.

6. School Rules

It wasn't a tractor. I rode between Vicki and Henry in Auntie Ed's beat-up pickup. Vicki drove and the butler held my borrowed backpack gingerly on his knees.

I had not won the argument, mostly because Clara hadn't packed any of my schoolwork. It was still under my bed in Chicago, but if Henry found out, it would be FedExed, so I didn't tell him.

By the flagpole in front of the school, Henry eased out of the truck and held the door for me. Maribeth waved at me from the front steps. Henry would have followed me, but Vicki stopped him.

"Phoebe needs to do this on her own, Henry," she told him.

"But—" said Henry, clearly torn.

"Give Phoebe the backpack and get back in the truck. You can't follow two steps behind her all day with a tray of refreshments. Relax, she'll be fine. It'll even be good for her, like broccoli."

Henry looked at me. He knows how much I hate the B-vegetable. I gave Vicki a dirty look and took the backpack. "I'll try it, just for today."

"Class, this is the new student I told you about," said the teacher. "I'd like you to welcome Phoebe Marchant. Phoebe comes to us all the way from Chicago, Illinois." She pointed it out on a map.

It might have been light-years away. Mrs. Latinsky's class was nothing like the Swiss boarding schools I read about in orphan books. And unlike Miss Edgecombe's School for Girls, Cecilia P. Wainwright Elementary had boys, too. To me, they were members of an alien species, but on the whole, interesting. Close by, a dark-haired girl with slightly crossed brown eyes sucked in her breath loudly.

"Phoebe, you'll sit here by Raquel," Mrs.

Latinsky continued, "up front." She led me to a seat beside the breath-sucker. To my relief, Maribeth sat down one row back on the left. As Mrs. Latinsky walked to her desk, Raquel whispered to the curly-haired girl next to her, who snickered in response. I caught part of the whisper: "Vicki . . . *People* magazine . . . millionaire . . . beans . . ." Other kids were looking now. I wanted to crawl off the microscope slide, to be a germ among billions. Being singled out for scientific inquiry wasn't fun.

I lied. "It wasn't me."

The curly-haired girl stared. Raquel abandoned her whispering. "It was! It's the same name! Your clothes are different, but it's you!"

"Don't believe everything you read," I whispered back. "I'm sure half of it was made up."

The boy behind me made a rude noise. "You gotta use Beano if you're gonna eat beans." He had evidently seen whatever Raquel had seen.

"Jimmy Wells, you cut that out. How could you say such a mean thing?" Maribeth whispered. Jimmy didn't answer, and Maribeth continued, clearly not expecting him to. "Pay no attention to him, Phoebe. He's an alien from Mars."

"Then he'll probably end up on the front page

of the *National Enquirer*," I replied. Maribeth giggled. Mrs. Latinsky shushed us, and we started the lesson.

"I have to eat this?" A thin woman wearing a hair net and a mean expression on her face had just handed me a cardboard tray with little compartments to keep the food separated. I couldn't identify the entrée, gravy-covered lumps of . . . ?

Maribeth stared doubtfully at her own meal. "Well, you can bring your own lunch—I mostly do that 'cause it's cheaper—but Mom said I should be helpful today."

At the end of the line, a fat woman sat behind a metal cash box. "That will be sixty-five cents," she told me.

"I'm sorry; I never carry money. Just send the bill to Henry," I replied. "He'll take care of it."

"That's okay, honey, you're new here," the cafeteria lady said. "You can bring it tomorrow." She fished a cracked red leather wallet from her purse and painstakingly counted out enough pennies, nickels, and dimes. "There, all set. Enjoy your lunch!"

"Phoebe, why don't you give Mrs. Turner an IOU?" Jimmy wisecracked. Behind him, Raquel nudged her friend and whispered in her ear.

"Do you really play Monopoly with real money?" the girl piped up.

Maribeth looked at her scornfully. "Sheesh. What kind of question is that? Who would play Monopoly with real money?"

Once we'd sat down, as far away from Jimmy as possible, Maribeth asked me, "I wonder why Raquel and Jimmy are acting like that. They never met you before, did they?"

"I guess they read about me," I answered her. "They read about my stepmother and they think they know me."

"Vicki? She used to be my baby-sitter when I was little. What'd she do? Rob a bank again or something?"

Again? I wanted to ask, but I also didn't want to answer any questions. "Or something." Then I corrected myself, not wanting to lie to Maribeth. "It's kind of hard to explain."

That seemed to satisfy Maribeth, or perhaps it was the butterscotch pudding that glued her mouth together, because she didn't ask any more questions about greediguts Vicki, and I didn't have to volunteer any more information. Raquel was staring at me again, so I looked cross-eyed back at her. She and the other kids didn't know anything, not about Henry, not about the anonymous trustee, not about that

68

crocodile-turned-lawyer, Mr. Grossbeak, who cared, in a sort of financial way. Judging from Maribeth's remark, they knew Vicki, though . . . A bank robber, huh? Maybe Henry would let me call Mr. Grossbeak now.

"Well, I think you're fine, Phoebe. Just the way you are," Maribeth declared loyally. "And if Jimmy says any different, I'll . . . I'll . . . well, I don't know what I'll do, but I'll think of something. So there!"

I felt warm inside. I'd remember this moment, when I was back in my cold city with real trees.

Just before the bell rang, Raquel sidled up and said, "Phoebe, why don't you come and sit with us tomorrow? I mean, you've got so much to learn about the school rules, and really, Phoebe, Maribeth doesn't know anything. I'll even prove it. Listen to this." Raquel put her hands on her hips. "Okay, Maribeth, who was the original Material Girl?"

Maribeth's bright blue eyes looked puzzled for a long moment. She hesitated before answering, "The Patchwork Girl of Oz?"

Raquel hooted. "Is that your final answer? It's Madonna, stupid!"

"Like, the rock star?" her friend added.

"Like I told you, Phoebe, you don't want to hang with her," Raquel finished.

Maribeth's face burned. Quickly I defended her. "I've read that book, Raquel, and I think it was a good answer. And, it's just fine with me if Maribeth shows me around."

Maribeth's grateful smile was all the payment I needed.

After lunch, the class trooped into the school library. "We've got twenty minutes to pick out books," Maribeth informed me.

I followed her example and picked out a stack of books, including one with a dragon on the cover that looked funny. They were heavy, though, and I struggled up to the checkout counter.

"If you would just call Henry at the Lazy V Ranch," I informed the woman in charge, "he'll see to it these are picked up." I pointed at Maribeth. "He'll take care of Maribeth's stack, too."

A lot of kids in Mrs. Latinsky's class must be not so distantly related to goldfish. They stood there staring, with their mouths open.

On the bus home, Jimmy Wells turned to me and said, "Do you want to go rock hunting? I know a cave where they used to mine stuff."

I looked at Maribeth. "What kind of 'stuff'?"

"Are you even allowed in there, Jimmy?" Maribeth asked.

"Sure, what's stopping us? Not Jessie Ann, I mean, you can't bring her, but the three of us can go."

"What kind of stuff?" I asked again.

Jimmy dug into his backpack. He dropped a fist-sized rock into my hand. "See, there's one I found. And there are lots more just like it, some even better than that."

I turned it over. It was your normal rock, grayish brown, but a streak of dark blue ran through it. "What is it?"

"That blue's azurite. The shiny bits are mica. Do you want to come see?"

Maribeth shrugged.

"Okay."

Maribeth, Jimmy, and I got off at the same bus stop by the Mullinses' ranch. "Meet me here in fifteen minutes," Jimmy said. He took off to the right, in the opposite direction of Auntie Ed's. Maribeth and I went inside her house. Maribeth dumped her schoolbooks out of her backpack, replacing them with a couple of water bottles and a flashlight. We found a note on the table from Maribeth's mother saying she had gone to town for groceries. Relieved of having to give any explanations and of Jessie Ann's tagalong curiosity, Maribeth added a note of her own.

Jimmy roared up on a three-wheeler soon afterward. Once across the road, a barbed-wire fence warned us away.

Jimmy held up the barbed wire as Maribeth and I ducked under. Maribeth returned the favor for Jimmy. The boy made a big production of getting his bearings, then set off. Pretty soon we were following the remains of a road. Here and there deep ruts paralleled where a wagon had once trundled. After a while we began to see rocks with some of the same bright blue specks along the way.

"You know," said Jimmy, a little too casually to be believed, "they say some stagecoach robbers once hid out in these parts."

"Really?" I said. "I guess that must have been a long time ago."

"Right," said Maribeth.

"I mean it," the boy protested.

"Who's 'they' then?" Maribeth demanded. "I've lived here all my life; you'd think I would have heard of it before."

Jimmy waved his hands, as if the air around them would bear witness to his story. "The two robbers had a disagreement and shot each other over a game of cards. One died right away; he was shot through the heart—"

"Jimmy, you're making this up." More used to the boy's stories, Maribeth looked skeptical.

"I'm not," Jimmy insisted. "It was in *Arizona Highways*. You can look it up. Anyway, the other one lingered for a few days, and when he was dying, confessed they'd hidden the gold somewhere in this area. He said he'd haunt the place, so's no one would ever find it. And"—here Jimmy paused dramatically—"to this day, nobody's ever found the gold, but I think it might be in the cave. I mean, it makes sense. They either had to bury it, or they had to hide it, and what better place than an abandoned mine? Gold is heavy, you know."

If we hadn't had Jimmy along to guide us, Maribeth and I would never have found the place, even with the best of directions. The mine lay to the right of the track, which still rambled westward, maybe all the way to California. The cave entrance was behind a big rock pile.

"Did you bring a flashlight?" Jimmy asked.

"Of course," said Maribeth. "Didn't you?"

He looked sheepish. "Dead batteries."

"Oh."

"You two go first. I'll be right behind you."

Getting down on our hands and knees, we entered single file like ants, Maribeth in front, with me right behind her.

"Do you think the stagecoach robbers had flashlights?" Maribeth whispered.

"Lanterns, for sure. They must've. How could they hide the treasure otherwise?" came Jimmy's answer behind me.

After about ten feet, the cavern opened up and we could stand. The air was cool in its shadows. Maribeth played her flashlight around the walls. Then she stopped. "Look, there's a petroglyph!" A small picture of a deer graced a relatively flat piece of rock. Even though it was just a crude outline, it looked like it was running.

"What's that?" I said.

"Ancient graffiti," Jimmy told me.

Wrinkling my nose, I said, "And what's that smell?"

"It wasn't me," said Jimmy. "It could have been, but it wasn't."

"I don't like this," said Maribeth, tugging on my shirttail. "I don't care if we don't find any pretty rocks. I *heard* something!"

Suddenly the flashlight began to dim, the dark coming closer. Just before it flickered out, I caught sight of glittering yellow eyes ahead.

Something moved. Someone screamed. I lit out of the cave as if my sneakers had been set on fire, Maribeth right behind me. Outside the entrance we yelled for Jimmy, but he didn't answer.

Looking at each other's frightened face, we turned and made tracks for the Lazy V.

The adults were on the porch. I grabbed Henry. "You've got to come quick! Jimmy's trapped in the cave!"

"Why, what happened to the two of you?" Vicki asked. She was busy patting Maribeth's arms, searching for broken bones.

"It's haunted," said Maribeth, her eyes huge in her pale face. "The ghost got Jimmy!"

"Which cave?" said Auntie Ed.

I explained. When I got to the part about the glittery eyes, Tim's shoulders started shaking and a rusty laugh escaped. His eyes watered and he had to wipe them with a bandanna. "I knew there was a family of javelinas living around here, and trust Jimmy to know where. Guess you spooked them good!"

I turned around. "You mean Jimmy knew those whatever-they-were lived in there?"

"Had to," said Tim. "That particular cave never had any good ore rocks."

Auntie Ed admonished him, "You know, Tim, it could have been a mountain lion. One's seen from time to time. I wouldn't want to box in a javelina either. And it isn't safe going into old mines. They often have drop-offs and open pits."

"There were a lot of eyes, Auntie Ed," I said, "and it smelled real bad in there."

"Javelinas, for sure," said Tim. And that rusty laughter started up again. The others joined in, even Henry.

"I'd better call Jimmy's mother, just to make sure he got home safe," said Auntie Ed. She headed inside. In a few minutes she was back. "She says he just roared up on his three-wheeler."

Maribeth struck out for home, vowing revenge. "Jimmy Wells got my goat. I'm going to get his someday!"

"I'm never being friends with a boy as long as I live. If Jimmy Wells were here right now, I'd run him over with his three-wheeler, flatten him out on the manure pile." I demonstrated with my hands.

"I've got a better idea," said Auntie Ed. "Come along with me."

I followed her into the kitchen. "And you did *not* have mountain lion on your predator list."

"Sometimes a new place is scary enough without adding a mountain lion," Auntie Ed observed.

"Or a whole herd of them!"

"You mean pack, Phoebe. Here, punch that down," the old woman directed.

"This?" A large mixing bowl covered with a checked towel stood on the counter.

Auntie Ed nodded. "Give it a good whack. Now we have to shape it into rolls, like this." She pinched off a piece of dough and rolled it into a ball. "Three of these'll make a cloverleaf roll, see?" She arranged them in a muffin tin.

I pinched off a piece. "This is Jimmy Wells's head."

"You don't want to work it too hard, or the rolls will be tough," Auntie Ed warned as I formed a few more balls of bread dough. "That's better."

We worked together steadily. Gradually, I dropped the grudge I'd been carrying, working the dough over instead.

Before Auntie Ed set the pan in the oven, she said, "It's nice having you here. Vicki was five when she first came to live here, a lot younger than you. But besides the age difference, you couldn't be further apart in a lot of respects. You're kind of standoffish, Phoebe, but I think you're only hiding behind stickers, like a cactus. Vicki, now, was just greedy for love, from that first day. I've missed her."

And, as an afterthought, "But, you know, one comes to love the cactus, too. Boys take longer." Auntie Ed winked.

7. What Do You Get When You Cross a Stepmother?

A week later things had settled more or less into a routine, as Henry and I adjusted to ranch rhythms. Vicki peeled off her city girl gloss. The red nails disappeared. She stuck a baseball cap on her head and wore her hair in a ponytail.

For my part I was quick to shed my fine silk dresses for some rougher and readier denims. Maybe my skin was getting tougher, too, because Vicki wasn't getting on my nerves quite so much. And even though I was still mad at Jimmy, I was coming to realize that in a small community, everyone mattered. Even though the news of our arrival had spread like wildfire, no photographers had shown up. A grudge could last a long time, true, but so could friendships. Mine with Maribeth appeared to be cementing.

And, yesterday, I'd gotten Lily to trot, just by squeezing my legs!

On the outside only Henry appeared unchanged, in his neatly pressed button-down shirts tucked precisely into belted trousers, never jeans. I knew he was used to being, well, useful, and initially fit in like fine china at a picnic—not at all. However, Auntie Ed was more than happy to surrender the cooking to him. Henry also kept in touch with Clara, Sal, and Porter back in Chicago. He ignored Vicki, maneuvering around her as though she'd been planted. He was polite, yet distant.

Late one afternoon after school, Auntie Ed trudged up the driveway. She held the mail in her arms, but she wasn't sorting the junk from the bills, the way she usually did.

"Someone bashed in the mailboxes. Again," she informed us. Vicki and I were relaxing on the porch, sipping lemonade Henry had made for us. Auntie Ed elaborated. "It's the third time that's happened. Well, I guess I'll drive into town and report it."

"Just call it in, Auntie Ed," advised Vicki. "I'll do it for you. Why don't you sit down for a second and join us? I'll zip in and get you a lemonade."

Auntie Ed shook her head. "No, it's got to be done. They pay more attention down at the sheriff's office if I show up. Privilege of age, I guess. Not that they ever catch who's doing it," she grumbled. "Oh, no." Auntie Ed went inside to get her truck keys.

"Maybe we can hammer out the dents," suggested Vicki, "if the damage isn't too bad. Come on, Phoebe, let's go investigate."

It looked like someone had swung a baseball bat down the line of mailboxes, starting with Auntie Ed's on the left end, then the Mullinses', then the Wellses', and five other neighbors'. None of them could be salvaged.

"Oh, too bad," said Vicki. "These were expensive. People can't be buying new ones all the time."

"You can't fix them?" I asked.

"No." Vicki thought for a moment, then she looked at me speculatively. "But, maybe we could together." On the way back to the ranch house, Vicki explained how having more money than you knew what to do with could be a good thing. "Tell Henry to grab the checkbook. Come down to the hardware store with me and I'll prove it."

*   *   *

As Vicki twisted the last screw into place, she said to me, "This is the opposite of vandalism—I'm not sure what you call it, though." She surveyed the row of shiny new mailboxes with pride.

"Well, I call it right nice," said Auntie Ed. She squeezed my hand.

Vicki was still talking about it at dinner. "This place needs something and it's easier to figure out problems in a small town. Not so overwhelming, like in the big city." She tapped a pencil against her front teeth. "It needs something and I'm going to get it figured out. Is it plain boredom, do you suppose? Hey, what if there was a place for kids and teenagers to hang out on Friday nights and all day Saturdays?"

"You mean so they don't go around whacking mailboxes for fun?" I asked.

"Right," said Vicki. "You've got it, Phoebe."

"This community needs something," agreed Auntie Ed. "Even the drive-in movie theater shut down. Not enough kids stay here, and who can blame them. They set their eyes on city lights and hightail it out of here once they graduate high school. Shoot, some don't even wait. They drop out and they're gone."

Vicki doodled on her notepad. "Well, Auntie Ed, what if this place I'm talking about was a place you could only go if you kept your grades up? Like a club. Would that be incentive enough?"

"Maybe, but, Vicki honey, where are you going to get the money? You always were a dreamer."

"It's important to dream, Auntie Ed. You know that. Anyway, I do have some money now. And don't forget, Phoebe's just sitting on barrels of money. All those beans. We can spend some and no one would ever miss it. Isn't it a good idea, Phoebe?"

I nodded. It did sound like fun, even coming from Vicki. "I'd like to help. We could have computers maybe. You could ask Mr. Grossbeak to set it up."

Vicki was taking notes. "We could have an old-fashioned soda fountain. Forty-six gazillion flavors of ice cream. No licorice, though. We could have—"

"Pie in the sky," Henry finished.

Vicki shot him a dirty look, then turned and smiled beatifically at me. "What's the point of being rich as what's his name—that king who turned everything to gold?"

"Midas," I said. I felt uncomfortable, remembering what had happened to Midas's daughter.

Everything he touched had turned to gold, even his own flesh and blood, before he learned his lesson. I'd forgotten how that story ended. Did his daughter stay hard and cold forever?

"Right, Midas, he's the man," agreed Vicki. "Well, what's the point if you can't have fun with it?"

Henry warned her she'd have to go through Mr. Grossbeak. "It isn't the kind of thing Mr. Albert would have done."

Vicki disagreed. "Bert was just getting around to it. Really."

Henry raised an eyebrow. "I think you'd ride down the street like Lady Godiva herself if it got you more money."

"Pooh, Henry, wouldn't you?"

Henry wouldn't. Anyone could see that.

"But then," Vicki pointed out, "your hair isn't long enough to cover up anything interesting."

Henry's face reddened at Vicki's comment. I couldn't tell if it was from embarrassment or anger. Maybe both.

Vicki hammered away at her point. "Henry, you'd think it was raining all the time the way you frown on everything. I'll bet—"

"I don't bet."

"No, you don't, do you? Well, if you're not

having fun, you might as well not live on this planet!"

"I just think you should think things through more," Henry protested. But Vicki had already left and he was arguing with the air.

Next afternoon the doorbell rang. Henry was nowhere in sight, so I answered it.

Two men, wearing shiny black suits and muted ties, their hands clasped respectfully in front of them, stood on Auntie Ed's big welcome mat. They were too well dressed to be reporters, so I relaxed. "Is your mother or father home, dear?" asked the older one.

"I think so. Just a minute," I said, unwilling to go into long explanations with strangers. I tracked down Henry in the kitchen, putting the finishing touches on a macaroni and cheese casserole. He trailed me to the door.

"Yes?" he said. "Mrs. Edna's not home. May I help you?"

"We're from Underhill's, sir. We've come to collect the remains of Henry Carr," said the man.

"The *what*?" said Henry. His jaw dropped. He looked from the men to the long black car sitting in the driveway.

"We're so sorry for your loss," the other man put in unctuously. "If you could just show us where the remains are, we'll take care of every—"

"But *I'm* Henry Carr!" Henry sputtered. "And I'm not dead!"

It took awhile to sort it all out, plus convince the undertakers that no one had really died. ("Yet," Henry muttered.) Mr. Underhill's ears perked up at this, and Henry had to say "Just kidding" through gritted teeth, and, eventually, the two men left, without Henry.

Henry had had to tip them for their troubles. He'd also had to make a contribution to the charity funeral fund. He looked at me. "Just where exactly is that stepmother of yours?"

"What're you going to do to her, Henry?" I asked.

"I don't know, but we may have to call Underhill's back. For real!"

We found Vicki in the barn, mucking out the stables. Henry stormed in, ignoring the impending destruction of his leather shoes.

Henry pointed a long narrow finger at my stepmother. "I suppose you're the one responsible for that little stunt."

"Why, whatever do you mean, Henry?" Vicki asked.

"The funeral home!"

"Oh, that particular little stunt—I thought you might be talking about . . . never mind." She turned innocent green eyes toward him. "Well, actually, I got the idea from Phoebe here."

My mouth hung open. A guilty conscience painted my cheeks. I started to back out of the barn. "I think I've got some homework . . ."

Henry turned the finger on me. "Stay right where you are, miss." I froze.

Vicki continued, "Yeah, you know, though? Crawly bugs aren't really my style and they're not so popular here—desert critters have their own protection defense systems just like cactuses have stickers. I didn't really want to hurt you, just like I know Phoebe would never want to hurt me. By the way, Phoebe, Sal is never going down the Amazon." I started guiltily. I had forgotten about the poison frogs. Vicki turned back to my butler. "But, Henry, you're so stiff, you're wearing your uniform even when you're not wearing it." She started shoveling again, aiming directly at Henry's shoes.

Henry left the barn abruptly. I trailed after him.

"And just what did Vicki mean, Miss Phoebe, when she said she got the idea from you?"

I traced my initials in the dirt with my toe. "I cannot tell a lie, George Washington. I suppose she meant the things I did to her back in Chicago. . . ." Then I had to spill it all out. "There were bugs—Vicki mentioned those—and then there was the bad hair thing that didn't work. I thought maybe I'd haunt her, so I borrowed Porter's spare set of snow chains for the limo and walked around, you know, clanking in the middle of the night. I could hardly lift them they were so heavy. I thought Vicki slept through all that groaning and moaning, but I guess she didn't. And—"

"Stop." Henry stared. "I'm surprised at you, miss." He tried to keep a straight face, but failed. "I am so surprised," he said. He had to sit down; he was laughing so hard. And suddenly, I was laughing, too, and Henry and I were sitting side by side in the dirt, holding our ribs.

Over dinner, Auntie Ed tried to look severely at her niece. "Vicki, how could you do it? That was really too bad of you."

"I just put a handkerchief over my mouth, and I cried into the phone. Oh, oh, oh," Vicki cried, holding her stomach, "I about busted my gut laughing!"

Henry wore a frosty air, but he couldn't ignore Vicki. No telling what she'd do next if he did.

I couldn't wait to find out.

I got my chance a few hours later. Eavesdropping is not polite, but sometimes it is necessary. Henry and Vicki were on the porch. I had flattened myself against the wall around the corner from them.

"Madam, I'm just saying it's wrong of you to spend Phoebe's money as if it were yours," I heard Henry say.

"Well, it's just a loan," Vicki said. "Like, for the pizzas? And I did pay for those later, you know."

"Oh?" Henry sounded surprised.

"Yeah, you can check with Mr. Grossbeak. It's on automatic debit from my checking account now."

"Well, you are still planning to spend money you don't yet have and you're influencing Phoebe to spend hers, too. This scheme of yours for a community teen center—while it may be a very worthy cause, I don't think it's right for you to spend Phoebe's money. She's not old enough to make decisions like that."

"Would you quit calling me madam? It's not like I wouldn't talk to Mr. Grossbeak and write to the other trustee, whoever he or she is, to get permission. I mean, I know I would need their approval, as well as Phoebe's. Henry, did you know that Bert never gave money to charity? Never!"

"I am aware of that." Henry sounded uncomfortable.

"And you think Phoebe should grow up to do the same, to be exactly like him?"

"I just think you are taking on too much."

"I am the girl's stepmother. Phoebe's got a lot of growing to do."

"I don't dispute that."

"And you are to Phoebe, exactly *what?*"

"I . . . I . . ." Henry didn't finish.

There was a pause. I strained to hear.

Vicki sighed. "You really think I'm such a bad influence, Henry?"

"I do."

"The trouble with you, Henry, is you are the kind of person who judges a book by its cover."

It got quiet after that and my stomach started to hurt. I waited five minutes, then went inside.

Creeping into Henry's room, I took the cell

phone from his briefcase. Then I retrieved Mr. Grossbeak's business card from my purse and locked myself in the bathroom. Because I didn't want anyone eavesdropping on my conversation, I started running water, so anyone going by would think I was scrub-a-dub-dubbing in the bathtub. I punched in the lawyer's number and pushed the button to connect us.

"Miss Phoebe, what can I do for you?" Mr. Grossbeak's voice sounded gravelly around the edges, as if I'd woken him up.

I didn't care. "You can make Vicki go away," I said. "Can you make her go away without me going to school in Switzerland? I want to come back to Chicago with Henry. Can you call that other trustee and decide it between the two of you?"

"Why, what's the matter? I talked to Henry just the other day, and he seemed reconciled to waiting out the six-week period stipulated in your father's will."

"Poppy wouldn't have wanted this, Mr. Grossbeak. I know it. They're fighting over me. I think Vicki wants Henry to leave, and I know he wants her to leave, and I want things to be the way they used to be!"

"I'm sorry, miss," he said gently. "With your father gone, you know they can't be that way. I'll speak to Henry in the morning; would that be sufficient?"

It would have to be, because he wasn't budging. I stuck the cell phone under my bed and pretended to be asleep, but I stayed awake a long time leaking tears on my pillow.

8. Bad Day Back at the Ranch

I jumped off the last step of the school bus, raising dust with my sneakers. My shirt stuck sweatily to my shoulder blades. The bus driver swung the door shut without saying good-bye.

It figured.

It had been the worst day. Maribeth had been having her braces tightened in the morning and Jimmy and Raquel had made the most of her absence. I had thought spitballs were only targeted at prim heroines in books written eighty years ago. I'd thought wrong; they were alive and well and zinging merrily through the air at Wainwright Elementary whenever Mrs. Latinsky looked the other way.

Then, I didn't have my lunch money again, and this time Mrs. Turner the cafeteria lady wasn't buying any excuses—or any soggy pizza apparently. "I'm sorry I can't give you any more credit, dear," she explained. "Not until Friday—that's my payday. Maybe someone will share with you."

"Come on, it's only sixty-five cents," I pleaded.

Mrs. Turner did her impression of Mt. Rushmore, face impassive, her will hard as rock (though her chins wobbled). "I'm sorry, dear. I just don't have it. If I did, I would lend it to you."

I couldn't believe it. "You must be kidding. Don't you get it? Don't you know who I am?" I stood up tall. "It's me—Phoebe Marchant—possibly the richest girl in the whole US of A! I'm the Bean King's daughter!"

Jimmy, in line to buy milk, piped up, "Phoebe, don't worry, I'll sell you half a ham and cheese sandwich for five dollars, at five thousand percent interest compounded daily." He whipped out his calculator and started punching buttons furiously. "Let's see, at the end of today, you'll owe me . . ."

I rounded on him. "You are *so* not helpful, Jimmy Wells. You, too, Mrs. Turner. Maybe you should try skipping a meal. You could save

94

a little money that way and you could certainly stand to lose some weight. Thanks for nothing!"

I heard a gasp behind me, and whirled, only to see Maribeth turn away. I could only watch as she deserted me to sit with Jessie Ann's kindergarten class. Well, fine! What did it matter? I would go back to Chicago in a few weeks, and who cared about some dumb Arizona kid. Who cared at all?

Well, maybe I did, though I wasn't ready to admit it. The hurt and anger had crawled into my stomach and were duking it out.

I stomped into the kitchen and slammed my backpack down on the table. Red-faced with effort, Henry was hand whipping some kind of brown goop with an eggbeater. "My kingdom for some KitchenAid appliances," he joked.

"Is there any lemonade?"

Henry nodded at the refrigerator. "In there. Auntie Ed made some fresh at lunchtime."

I didn't need reminding about lunchtime. "Can you get me some?"

"Not right now. I'm making a chocolate cake for dessert. It's right there, top shelf. Help yourself."

I stared at Henry. "No! You get it!"

Henry stopped cranking and narrowed his eyes at me. "What's biting you? Vicki slip a tarantula in your backpack?"

At the mention of my stepmother, the bane of my existence, she who made me pick up my own socks *and* wash them, I burst into tears. Appalled, Henry abandoned the cake batter. He patted me awkwardly on the shoulder, but I was in no mood to be comforted.

"I want to go back to Chicago!" I yelled. "I want things to be the way they used to be."

"It's only a few more weeks," Henry soothed. "I thought you liked it here. Don't you have Maribeth? And me?"

"You only look after me because you're paid to do it!" The words flew from my mouth before I could clip their wings. They hovered in the air between us.

"Is that what you think?" Henry looked like he'd been gut shot. He opened his mouth to say something more, then closed it. He turned and walked away.

"Wait!" I cried. "Wait, Henry!" But Henry had erected a stone wall around himself. I could only stand and watch as the mortar set.

But I found I couldn't, after all. Not with Henry. Never with Henry.

Turning, I ran. I ended up in the hay barn,

perched on one bale, leaning up against another. It was hot, dusty, and scratchy. It was miserable, but then, so was I. One tear, and then another followed, chasing down my cheeks.

Finally, cried out, I climbed down. Arms folded across her chest, Vicki waited for me on the porch.

"Do you want to tell me why Henry's packed his bags?" She read the answer on my face. "Girl, you'd better listen to me. I'm not getting ten million bucks to be your baby-sitter, you know."

"You're not my mother! You can't tell me anything!"

"No, but I'm as close as you'll ever get unless Henry has a sex change! Look, Phoebe, he's a proud man, and he doesn't like his character being questioned. What did you say to him?" When I didn't answer, she said, "Honey, your daddy may have thought he was protecting you by keeping you in mothballs, but that isn't the case. Now, I don't think Henry will listen to me, but he might—I say *might*—listen to you if you went and apologized."

At the mention of Poppy, my stomach hurt even worse. I didn't think I had any more tears in me, but it turns out I did. I blinked hard to hold them back. I realized that without Henry, there would be an even bigger, blacker hole in my life. Henry had always been there. He had to be there. Without Henry, what would I do? The tears gushed out, and I couldn't hide them from Vicki.

"Come here, Phoebe," said my stepmother. She reached for me. At first I resisted and stood stiffly, but then I let go and the tears got her front wet, too. Vicki held me close without speaking for a long time. Finally she let go.

"I'm lower than a snake," I told my step-mother, unconsciously copying Maribeth's manner of speaking.

Vicki's mouth twitched a bit, but she said, "You'll have to crawl a lot lower than a snake, but I think you can do it. Henry loves you, you see."

"He does?"

"You can actually doubt it?" Vicki gave me a push on the shoulder. "Why else would he put up with you? Go on, get him to put his socks back neatly in the drawer."

I headed inside, wishing I felt bolstered by Vicki's words. Instead I felt like a scarecrow with half her straw stuffing fallen out.

It was quiet inside the ranch house, and dark, with the windows shuttered against the afternoon sun. Once my eyes adjusted, I headed down the hallway and knocked on Henry's door.

Auntie Ed came out. "Are you looking for Henry? He's not here. He asked me if I could spare Tim for a few hours to drive him into town."

I didn't want to believe her.

I turned the knob and pushed the guest room door open. The bed was neatly made, but Henry always left it like that. It told me nothing. I rushed to the dresser and yanked open the top drawer.

Empty.

9. Making It Right

Vicki drove me to the airport in Mrs. Mullins's minivan, which you would never have guessed could do better than eighty miles an hour on a straightaway. Concentrating on the road ahead, my stepmother kept quiet, which must have been a strain. She parked in the short-term lot and set off at a brisk pace, an advertisement for the power of positive thinking. But what if I was too late?

Vicki checked with a woman at the ticket counter. We headed down the hallway to the gates, the carpeting stretching out forever in front of us like a gray oily sea. At first, my eyes scanned past him, because he didn't look like Henry. He was slumping—Henry never slumped—in a chair in the departure lounge. He

100

was staring straight ahead, but he didn't see us. I don't think he saw anything.

Vicki gave me a nudge. "I'll be waiting. Take as long as you need."

I stepped forward. "Henry?"

He didn't look up. I stayed standing, twisting my fingers together. "Henry, would you look at me? I need to talk to you." And I needed to say more, I knew that, but my tongue wouldn't perform, the words sticking to my teeth.

He kept his eyes stubbornly focused on the carpet.

I stamped my foot. No way would he ignore me. "Henry, you can't go back to Chicago without me. You just can't! You know your place is here with me."

"Why? Because it's my job?" He looked up and his eyes bored into mine. His question hung in the air, and I knew I'd made a tactical error. Henry continued, "And if I don't? What, you'll fire me? Well, maybe I quit!"

I froze. Henry had never spoken to me this way. He couldn't quit. He wouldn't—would he? "But, I . . . I don't want you to go."

Henry broke the chilly silence. "I'm not sure we can make this work, miss."

"I want to try, Henry. Please, will you let me try? And, please, won't you stop calling me miss?"

He drew in a ragged breath. "Phoebe, when we came here, I saw it not as a place to hide, but as a place to heal, a place to let you be . . ." He was hesitating over words. ". . . A place to let you be yourself. Not surrounded by everything."

"But, I won't ever be a regular kid, Henry! You know I can't ever get away from it."

"By 'it,' I presume you mean the money?" he asked softly.

I nodded. "It's kind of like a tattoo on my forehead; it doesn't go away and everyone can see it."

"Truthfully, Phoebe, don't you use the fact of your inheritance to your advantage? When it suits you?"

I looked down at the carpet, which was still the same horrid color. "I suppose." Certainly it made me think I somehow deserved movie star treatment. But then, there was the other side of the coin, too: that no one could possibly love me for myself.

With Henry, though, it had been different.

While I digested this thought, he went on. "People have formed an impression of you."

"Yes, they have," I said in a small voice. "Especially this afternoon, they have very much formed an impression of me."

"And you can change that impression if you try hard."

"Please, Henry . . ." I whispered.

A loudspeaker voice interrupted me, announcing final boarding for Chicago. "All passengers should be at gate twenty-seven." Henry stood up.

If he picks up his briefcase, I will make like a gila monster and glom onto his trouser knees and bite his black shoes, and never let loose, I will—

Henry picked up his briefcase.

I would even beg. "Please I need you."

Henry's hands on my shoulders felt like goodbye. "Listen to me, Phoebe. You could be penniless, but what counts is your true worth. Don't ever let your money substitute for you. For the real Phoebe." He hesitated. "For the Phoebe I couldn't do without." At the last, I was in his arms faster than the wind could whistle.

"I'm so sorry, Henry." And later, "You won't get on the plane, will you?"

He raised his eyebrow. "You can't fire me and I can't quit. Are we agreed?"

I hugged him harder. Then my horrible day spilled out: Jimmy calculating his compound interest, the porkulent cafeteria lady I had insulted. "I mean, she could have a glandular problem, Henry, or maybe Twinkies are Mrs. Turner's favorite food in the whole world. It doesn't matter; I said some awful things."

And, anyway, then there was Maribeth. That stony hurt in her blue eyes before she'd turned and walked away. "She's going to hate me forever, Henry."

Henry asked the right questions, listened hard, and let me come up with the answers. When I had settled on what I was going to do, I had Henry's approval.

Vicki was waiting by the exit. She had a big bag of M&Ms, which she put into my hands. "Thought you all could use some chocolate, but don't eat those mutant blue ones," she said. "I'll take care of those. You know, some days you absolutely need chocolate. Come on, I'll drive you back."

I fell asleep leaning against Henry's shoulder.

Vicki let Henry and me know what she thought after dinner. "I think that this is not working. I don't want to come between you two. Though it hurts to admit it, Henry was right all along. You two go on back to Chicago, and I'll stay here." She patted her aunt's hand. "Auntie Ed needs me closer than Chicago."

"It has been nice," said Auntie Ed. "I've missed you, Vicki." She put her blue-veined hand on top of her niece's. "I find I don't miss the quiet."

"But," I started to protest.

Vicki didn't let me interrupt. "No, you don't need me, Phoebe. You have Henry, who thinks I'm a bad influence; maybe I've thought the same way about him at times. Anyway, I know I embarrass you. I'm like training wheels, you know? Once you get your balance you don't need them anymore."

Henry didn't say anything. He just stared at Vicki, like she'd changed from a golden coach into a pumpkin before his very eyes. Finally, he asked, "You're giving up ten million dollars?"

"Yeah, I ought to have my head examined, huh?" Vicki's tone was joking, but her eyes weren't. "Give it away if you don't have any use for it, Phoebe. That's what I was going to do. There's lots of places that could use it well. Maybe Mr. Grossbeak would help you."

There was silence. Finally, I thought of something. "But you promised to take me to the county fair." I knew I sounded like Jessie Ann at her whiniest, but it was all I could come up with on short notice.

"I did, didn't I?" Vicki mused. "Well, it opens in two days. I'll keep my promise. You two can get a flight out afterward."

Auntie Ed headed for the living room and her favorite television show. I left Henry and Vicki alone with the dirty dishes. The only sound was the clink of silverware and the rattling of plates because Henry and Vicki weren't saying anything to each other.

I escaped from their silence to my room. I lay on the bed and buried my face in Fred's fur. As if I'd pushed an *on* button, he started his motor. Cats were simple, stupid. You always knew what they'd do. Not like people. It was strange, what people would do for money, strange what they wouldn't do.

I'd thought I had Vicki all figured out. I'd treated Henry badly and almost lost him. Unless I could make it up to her somehow, I'd lost Maribeth.

Once upon a time—okay, even last night—I'd wanted my stepmother gone, out of my life.

Now I wasn't so sure. I had an idea of Vicki in my head, but it didn't quite mesh with the real woman. I remembered my promise to Poppy, to try. Maybe up until now, I'd concentrated on what would happen if I didn't try. But, even more than I did not want to be sent away, I now wanted my six weeks with Vicki. She had helped me with Henry. It was only fair.

How could I make her change her mind?

10. Peace Talks

Right after breakfast I ran next door.

Maribeth was in the pen with her goats, Tarzan and Jane. Their mother, Mrs. Tootles, was chewing contentedly on some hay, thinking about whatever goats think about. Certainly they don't have problems like mine.

"Hi," I said.

Maribeth looked up but didn't say a word. Her blue eyes frosted over into a glacial stare.

"I did a dumb thing," I told her. "I didn't think." I rushed on. "I've gotten so used to being the center of everything, and getting my way, that I just—well, I got mad and said something I shouldn't have."

Maribeth said, "Mrs. Turner gained all that

weight last year, after her husband had a heart attack and died. If someone like Raquel had said it to her, well, I might have understood, but you, Phoebe, I don't know . . ."

"I'm really sorry. I didn't know about Mr. Turner. Maybe you could help me figure out how to make it up to her?"

Maribeth got up to leave. "You're so smart at insulting people, you figure it out."

I touched her arm, but she shrugged me off. "Please."

I had never understood how one word could be magic before, but somehow it melted the ice in Maribeth's eyes.

"Well . . . You'll have to apologize," the girl declared.

"Yes."

"And it'll have to be sincere."

"I know. It will be. And I'll have to make it up to Jimmy, too."

Maribeth looked at me. "I don't know if I'd go that far."

"But won't Vicki miss you and change her mind?" Maribeth was still trying hard to make me feel better, while we waited for the bus.

"Huh, not likely. She doesn't see me as anything but spoiled."

Maribeth didn't give up easily. "Phoebe, like when Candace's parents split, and they wanted her to choose between them, and she just couldn't. And she stopped eating and got so skinny. I think she tried to absolutely make herself disappear. Vicki and Henry seem like they want you to make a choice between them, but Vicki's not going to let you make it—she's made it for you."

I squeezed Maribeth's hand. "Yes, you're right. I'll be okay." Eventually, like Candace had. I wouldn't need to get used to it, if I could just convince Vicki to let us stay. At least for six weeks, as Poppy had wished.

I thought out loud. "Maybe if I . . . no . . ." I'd talk to the shiny line of new mailboxes, if they'd give me an answer.

Jimmy slouched over, backpack hanging off one shoulder. "Hi, Phoebe." He smirked. "Feeling better?"

I narrowed my eyes. I was definitely not falling for his politeness routine. "Not when I get a good look at you, Jimmy."

The bus pulled up with a screech of brakes and the three of us hopped on. Jimmy sat behind us. I put a finger to my lips. Maribeth nodded her agreement.

"From the looks of you two, it must be true that money can't buy happiness," observed

Jimmy in a stage whisper. Then thankfully he shut up.

During class time, Maribeth and I couldn't talk, but after school we did, as we wiped down the tables in the cafeteria with a mild bleach solution. Mrs. Turner looked on approvingly. It hadn't been as hard as I'd thought it would be to apologize to her. I'd only had to say the words, "I'm sorry," and Mrs. Turner had given me a hug. Then she'd given me a job, putting me to work cleaning up the cafeteria.

"How about we put Henry up on Lily, then he falls off and breaks his leg?" I suggested.

"Ouch! Phoebe, that would hurt! And he might not break his leg. Then he'd be suspicious," Maribeth pointed out.

"Yeah. But he'd have to stay over for a few more weeks."

"Not if it was his arm instead. Can't you think of something nonviolent?"

Trouble is, I couldn't. Maybe I'd been watching too much TV. Vicki's crazy schemes Auntie Ed had half told me about—the underwear catapult, the double amputee frogs, the buried treasure map—I needed one of those right now. Something fantastic. Something Henry couldn't ignore.

Wait a minute . . . "Maribeth! I think I have an idea."

Later that afternoon, we snuck into Henry's room. "You're sure he's not around?" Maribeth said, looking over her shoulder at the door. Clearly, she expected Henry to walk in and catch us red-handed. And what possible explanation could we give for going through his drawers? We'd be dead meat, for sure.

"Pooh, Maribeth. He went grocery shopping with Auntie Ed. He carries the coupons for her. They'll be at it for a while."

"Where's Vicki then?"

"I don't know exactly, but you can bet she's not coming anywhere near Henry's room. They're not talking to each other except very politely when it's absolutely necessary. I have to go with Henry when he leaves for Chicago, unless this works. Open the pillowcase."

Maribeth dutifully held open the pillowcase, and I crammed Henry's clothes into it. Thinking of Lady Godiva, I said, "I'll leave his underwear and socks, though."

"What about the sheets?" Maribeth asked.

"What about them?"

"You know, the Romans. Or was it the Greeks? Anyway, the ones that wore sheets."

"You mean like togas?"

"Yeah, togas."

"Yeah, we'd better take those, too," I agreed. As we left, I wondered aloud, "Do you think there's any way we could lock the door from outside?" Well, maybe it wouldn't be necessary. Henry wasn't likely to come out wearing only his boxers and socks. He'd have to stay put.

When Vicki tracked me down after Maribeth went home, I was reading a book on my bed, Henry's clothes tucked out of sight under it. I was trying to lose myself in Jane Eyre's problems to avoid thinking of my own.

"Phoebe," Vicki said, "come here for a second. I have something to give to you. I was going to wait, but . . . Well, since after tomorrow we probably won't be seeing each other, I'll give it to you now."

"What is it?"

"Something your father gave me, for you." Vicki rustled through her top drawer, pulled out a file folder, and thumbed through the papers inside. "Here it is."

She handed me a small photo, just a snapshot of a woman laughing at whoever was taking her picture. She was dressed casually, in jeans and a sweater. She had blue eyes and brown hair that could have used a comb. She could have been one of the moms at school, except she was over-dressed for the desert weather.

"Who is it?"

"You don't know? When Bert told me you'd never seen a picture of her, I didn't believe him. I do now. It's your mother, Phoebe."

I stared harder, looking for the resemblance. Maybe in the eyes, in the color of her hair. I was greedy for any details that would prove I'd belonged to someone once.

"Bert kept this to himself, for a long time, for the wrong reasons. She loved you, and so did your father. I know he would have wanted what's best for you," Vicki explained, "and that's what I'm trying to do, Phoebe."

"But I don't want to go!" I cried.

Vicki drew in a ragged breath. "You'll be fine, Phoebe. You've got a lot of good people to look after you. Especially Henry. You'll be fine."

As Vicki left the room, she told me, "The picture is yours, of course. You'll keep it safe, I know."

I looked back at the picture. My mother. She didn't look like one of the stepmothers. She looked . . . nice. She looked like someone a girl could love. Who had loved me, Phoebe, just for myself. If I could only remember.

Vicki stuck her head back in. "And put Henry's clothes back in his room, will you?"

I jumped up guiltily. "How did you know?"

"I've been playing tricks since before you were born, honey. You can't fool me."

"I did leave his underwear. Please," I pleaded.

Vicki shook her head. "He already thinks I'm a bad influence. If he sees all his clothes gone, he'll *know* it. Besides, you need to think these things through better. He would just wear the pants he wore today, or borrow from Tim." Vicki lowered her voice. "You need to think a little more creatively. Itch powder, for instance."

"Itch powder?" I asked hopefully. "Where do I get some of that? I could put it in all his underwear."

"No way, Phoebe. I'm staying out of it. You two have plane reservations after the fair and I'm driving you to the airport myself. Please, Phoebe, don't make this harder than it already is. May I have your promise?"

"Okay," I whispered. "No flat tires, no missing car keys."

Vicki waited.

"No cactus stickers in anyone's underwear, I promise."

"That about covers it, I guess," said Vicki.

"But, Vicki," I said, "what are you going to do for money without me? What about your plans for a place for teenagers with good grades and too much time on their hands? Did you think about that?"

Vicki looked at me. "Yeah, I did think about that. But I'll find a way. I'm a resourceful person. And Bert left me that stipend."

"Maribeth told me you robbed a bank once."

"She told you that?" Vicki laughed. "It's a good thing they don't send seven-year-olds to jail. You see, it was like this. There was a family begging outside the grocery store, and I wanted to help them. Auntie Ed said no, she didn't have enough money, so I thought about a place that had lots of money, and when we went there, I printed on the back of her deposit slip, carefully as I could: GIVE ME ALL YOUR MONEY."

I stared. "So, what happened?"

"Well, then Auntie Ed got arrested temporarily, there was a big fuss, and I got my picture in the paper. But guess what else happened?"

"What?" I said. I couldn't imagine.

"Seven people who read the article sent me money, and I got to use it to help that family. Another person offered the parents jobs, and so there was a happy ending to it all. Auntie Ed kept me on a very tight rein for a while after that, but the Turners loved me."

"The Turners? Like the lady who works at the school?"

"That's the one. Anyway, Phoebe, I guess my point is, I trust in something good to happen, and if I can have a hand in making it happen, I will."

Vicki left, before I could tell her Pollyanna would have loved her.

I tackled Henry after he and Auntie Ed returned with the groceries. "Come for a walk with me?"

"You go along, Henry," said Auntie Ed. "I can get the groceries put away myself."

We walked out into the desert, striking off at random. I waited until we were out of earshot of the ranch before speaking. "Please, Henry. Can't you say something to her? I want to stay with Vicki."

"Your stepmother's only after your money, Phoebe. You can see that, can't you?"

"Yes, I know that, but she's never pretended, Henry, not like the others."

"That's true. Your last stepmother's always been honest, in a greedy way."

Maybe money could buy happiness. "Do you think if I offered her more money, she'd let us stay?"

Henry snorted. "Vicki's pretty devious, but I don't think she's *that* devious. No, I think she's figured out it isn't going to work, so she's cutting her losses."

"You really think that?"

"To be honest with you, Phoebe, I don't know what to think. Her announcement over dinner last night was surprising, to say the least. You seem to think you can put up with her antics, but I'm not sure I can."

"Won't you do anything, Henry? Give her a second chance?"

He stopped. "Has she become that important to you, Phoebe?"

"Yes, Henry, I think she has. If I don't have something to laugh about, I might as well be an old, dried-up, well, an old, dried-up bean."

Henry put his hands on my shoulders. "I wouldn't want that to happen to you. Tell you what, Phoebe. I'll try to bend a little. We're going to the fair tomorrow. You go off with your friends, and I'll talk to Vicki."

I jumped up and down. "Oh, Henry, I knew you would!"

"Wait a minute." Henry put his hands in the air, protesting. "I'm not promising. I just said I'd talk to her. And for once I'll listen to what she has to say. But don't count on anything changing. Sometimes things can't be fixed."

"A lot of people say that, Henry, but you

know what? There's a lot that can be fixed, if you just apply your brain to the problem."

"Who told you that?"

"Oh, just a bank robber I know."

I held Henry's hand and we walked back to the ranch house.

11. The Missing Link Revealed

From a crane, the bungee chair of death dangled high over our heads. If you took a porch swing, added seat belts, and attached it to a giant slingshot, that's what you'd get. Air bags would probably come in handy, too.

Maribeth, Jimmy, and I were at the county fair. Each of us had money, a meeting place to catch up with wandering grown-ups, and several glorious hours without them. The thrill of midway rides awaited. I could just glimpse the top of the giant Ferris wheel, all lit up and spinning slowly.

That compensated. I hadn't been able to get Vicki to change her mind. And my last-ditch emergency call to Mr. Grossbeak had proved fruitless.

"Changing Mrs. Marchant's mind is not my job," the lawyer had explained, muttering something about Vicki's need for a brain transplant. Then came a rasping noise in my ear. After a moment I realized he was trying to make a joke, though it wasn't funny to me.

"Can't you offer her more money? Like twenty million?"

I hardly had to imagine his eyebrows flying up in shock, but his answer was unequivocal. That hadn't been my father's intention, and it would be "abdicating his financial responsibility toward the estate" to do any such thing. All those big words were just a long way of saying no.

I don't give up easily. "Well, would you just talk to the other trustee, you know, the one who would rather remain nameless and send quarterly anonymous postcards to that Swiss boarding school? Please, Mr. Grossbeak!" I was practically begging.

Mr. Grossbeak said the anonymous trustee was aware of the situation, and that there was nothing else that could be done. I would have argued some more, but I knew it wasn't just a matter of money or undue influence.

Vicki didn't want to come between Henry and me. She'd made that clear. Still, there had to be a way to get Vicki to let us stay on at the Lazy V, or to talk Vicki into flying back to Chicago with us, but I was absolutely out of clever ideas. For now, anyway, I had to leave it alone. Vicki and Henry had disappeared after setting a time and place to meet for dinner. Maybe they would actually talk to each other, and Henry had promised to try, so that was a good thing. Until then, it wasn't any use worrying. Again, I remembered one of my favorite book orphans, Pollyanna, and her "Glad" game. Pollyanna the eternal optimist would be hard pressed to find any good here. Still, I might as well follow Pollyanna's example and quit worrying.

That, or bungee jump into oblivion. *Boing!*

"I'd do it," said Jimmy, still mesmerized by the bungee contraption.

"Yeah, right," said Maribeth. She rolled her eyes. "You would not."

"I would," Jimmy said. "I just don't have the money. It costs a lot." He glanced in my direction. "I guess you wouldn't do it, would you?"

His implication stung, but not enough for me to make like a crazy human projectile. The notion that I could do anything because of all the money my father had left me was beginning to irritate. It actually meant I just had to make a lot more choices. I kept my mouth shut, however, and Maribeth and I headed toward the midway.

Jimmy trotted after us, but Maribeth stopped him. "Get lost, Jimmy. Go bother someone else." Just to be contrary, Jimmy dogged our heels for a few more minutes, but he peeled off by the petting zoo.

"All clear, Mission Control," I intoned.

Maribeth grinned her agreement. "Is this going to be fun or what? What do you want to do first?"

A little boy walked by. He had hold of a cloud of cotton candy almost as big as he was. He grabbed a sticky wad and stuffed it in his mouth.

"Mmm . . . that," I pointed. I bought a blue cotton candy, Maribeth a pink. The spun sugar melted when it touched my tongue, like a sweetened snowflake, though it wasn't cold at all.

The mysterious house of mirrors lured us first. However, too many fingerprints on the glass gave it away, and I only bumped my nose once. The fun houses were my favorites. Stepping onto whirling circles, divided stairs, with my left foot going down just as the right came up. Maribeth's favorite was the giant slide. At the top, you flopped onto a piece of burlap sacking, then screamed all the way down. Maribeth wouldn't try any rides that spun you around in circles.

"Throw-up rides," she said, but then she added generously, "you throw up if you like."

I said I'd rather ride the bumper cars.

Then we roamed among the game stalls, stopping to play the water balloon race. I stood behind my water gun and lined its sight on the clown's mouth. I pulled the trigger, ready. When the bell rang, I had won a small stuffed lion made in Taiwan. His eyes were crossed, and he only grew whiskers on the left side of his nose.

"Try again, lucky lady?" said the woman running the game. "Get one twice as big if you win."

"No, thanks."

Most of the other games Maribeth and I judged a waste of money—at least, we didn't think we had a chance to win them. We pointed ourselves toward the animal barns.

In the main barn, 4-H kids were showing sheep and we stopped to watch. Freshly shampooed sheep paraded in a circle around the judges. Their owners, mostly girls with neat French braids, wore green vests with little string ties, over white pants so clean they looked like they'd been dry-cleaned. To Maribeth's left, a woman was earnestly telling another how sheep kept teenagers from getting pregnant.

"My daughter came home from school and said she wanted a baby. So, I bought her two lambs, stuck them in her room, with bottles, and said, 'Here you are.' After three days she was begging to get them out of there—chewing on her hair at three o'clock in the morning, bawling for milk, never mind what they did to mess up her floor. We moved them to the barn. She didn't say anything about babies after that. And now look!" She beamed with pride as her daughter's sheep received a blue ribbon.

Giggling, Maribeth poked me. "Bet they don't teach that in health next year."

"So, when do they judge Tarzan and Jane?" I asked.

"Oh, that's tomorrow afternoon."

"Are you nervous?"

"A little," Maribeth admitted. "They're a bit on the small side, being twins. But, I think they show well. Can you come watch?"

I shook my head. "Henry and I've got plane tickets back to Chicago, remember? Not unless I can convince Vicki to let us stay."

Maribeth stayed silent for a moment. "Oh, I was trying to forget." Then she brightened. "Tomorrow is another day, Scarlett O'Hara."

I hesitated. "Can I ask you something, Maribeth?"

"Course, Phoebe, we're friends. And we're going to stay that way!"

"Yeah." I wished I could be as certain. "Maribeth? Well, once you asked me about Vicki. You asked if she'd robbed a bank or something, if that's why she was in the papers."

"I know why she was in the papers, doofus. My mom told me."

"Yeah," I persisted, "but why would you think she'd rob a bank? Again, I mean. I know about the first time."

Maribeth looked at me cockeyed. "Same reason. To give the money away!"

"Like Robin Hood?"

"That's right. That guy who robbed from the rich to give to the poor? Unless your dad made Vicki feel real sorry for him, my mom says there's no way she would have married him otherwise." She stopped. "Oh, I'm sorry, Phoebe, I heard about your dad, I forgot he . . . oh, I'm sorry. I didn't mean it. That's just the way Vicki is. Friends?"

"Friends," I agreed, taking a deep breath. "It's okay."

"Now come on, let's check out Tarzan and Jane's competition," Maribeth said. At the end of the enclosures, she nudged me. "Hey, look at that."

Inside Maribeth's assigned goat pen, Henry and Vicki sat side by side on a bale of hay. Jane was chewing on Henry's shoelaces, but he didn't appear to notice. Henry was holding Vicki's hand, and Vicki was crying. It wasn't pretty—her nose was swollen, her mascara had laid tracks down her cheeks. Henry looked pale and shaky. Suddenly he looked up. He stood, ran, and vaulted over another couple bales of hay to get to me.

He grabbed me hard by the shoulders, his eyes wide.

"What? What's wrong, Henry?"

"Phoebe, you're safe!"

"Yeah, I decided not to go bungee jumping, but I almost lost my lunch on the Tilt-a-Whirl anyway. Why are you crying, Henry?"

"We thought we'd lost you!"

Now Vicki was walking toward us, carefully putting one step in front of another, as though balanced on the high wire. "It's really you?" She put her arms around me tentatively, as if I might disappear.

"What's going on?" Maribeth demanded.

"You see, we thought you'd been kidnapped," Henry said quietly.

"Kidnapped?" My voice came out all squeaky.

"We found this," Vicki explained, holding up a piece of paper. "It was tacked onto the enclosure." She read aloud. "IF YOU WANT TO SEE YOUR

KID AGAIN PUT ALL YOUR MONEY IN A SACK AND LEAVE IT BY THE CAVIES."

"I still don't know what cavies are," said Henry, "but I do know I was scared to death when I read that note." He pulled me into a tight hug. "I'm glad you're all right."

"They're carrot hogs—guinea pigs, Henry," I explained.

"So, I still don't get it—what is that note about?" Henry asked. "You obviously weren't kidnapped. Was it just a sick joke, or has someone else been kidnapped? Someone somebody thought was you? We've got to go to the police if that's the case."

"Hold on," I said slowly. "I think I know what happened, and I bet I know who's behind it. It wasn't a person kidnapped, Henry, but it was a kid."

Maribeth was looking behind hay bales. "My kid!" wailed Maribeth, "my baby goat! We've got to get Tarzan back."

"This is about a goat?" Henry started laughing, and tears of relief streamed down his cheeks. He brushed them away. "Sorry, I can't help it. In that case, we'd better call in the FBI."

"Tell us everything," coaxed Vicki. "We'll get him back, Maribeth." She sat down heavily on a hay bale. "I haven't had this much excitement since the tiger escaped from the circus."

I looked suspiciously at Vicki. Somehow it didn't sound like a figure of speech. I'd have to ask later.

After we found Tarzan.

First, we checked the other goat enclosures. Jimmy was lazy, and that would be an easy hiding place.

"They all look alike to me," admitted Henry.

"He's not in any of these," Maribeth said. "I'm positive."

"What if you put Jane on a leash? Couldn't she track him down?" I asked Maribeth. "You know, like a bloodhound?"

"Jane won't even walk in a straight line, Phoebe. That won't work."

"What about the petting zoo?" suggested Vicki.

Maribeth looked hopeful. "Do you think?"

"It's got to be," I said. "You know Jimmy's going to want to go on rides, and how can he do that with Tarzan in tow?"

Describing Jimmy thoroughly, we stationed Henry on guard by the guinea pigs. Then the three of us beelined it to the petting zoo, past the zebra with a sign that said WHOA, I BITE!

Over in a corner Tarzan was nibbling delicately on a handful of corn held by a giggling toddler. He pushed closer, switching over to sample the ruffles of her dress.

"Oh, Tarzan!" said Maribeth. She gave him a quick, fierce hug.

Vicki talked to the attendant, then came over. "Let's get him out of here."

Back in the animal barn, a subdued Jimmy was sitting on a bench. Arms folded across his chest, wearing his best butler's sneer, Henry towered over him. He nodded at Maribeth and me, and raised one eyebrow. You want me to take care of him? his expression said.

I sat down on one side of Jimmy, Maribeth on the other, like bookends.

Then, casually, I offered, "I've got some money left over, Jimmy. How about if we watch you do the bungee swing? I've got plenty of money, you know. And since I know you want to do it, and you obviously really wanted it badly enough to kidnap Maribeth's baby goat, I figure I'd better give you some. Really, that's okay, I don't need it. We just want to watch when you do it."

Jimmy's face reddened. "Aw, that's okay, Phoebe, I don't need to do it."

"But, you obviously want to. Here, take it." I dug into the pocket of my shorts and fished out a wad of cash.

"Shoot, do it twice if you want to," Maribeth said.

"Really, it's okay." I still held out the cash, but Jimmy didn't make a move to take it.

"I don't want to do it, anyway," the boy muttered. Even the tips of his ears had caught fire.

"How noble of you," said Henry.

"Yeah, you don't want to pee in your pants in front of thousands," Maribeth jeered.

Jimmy slunk away. Maribeth ran after him. "Jimmy, you are paying for all the rides I want to go on! Starting right now!"

Somehow, I knew, come Monday at school, a certain Mr. Wells wouldn't be as much of a pain. If only I could be there to see it.

The goat-napping led to another discovery. I remembered Henry's face when I came into the pen. All at once I knew the truth. Whirling on him, I exclaimed, "You're the other trustee! You are, aren't you?"

Henry struck a pose, George Washington crossing the Delaware River, with goats milling around him. "I cannot tell a lie. I am the trusty trustee."

Vicki's mouth hung open.

"Don't look so surprised, Vicki. Who else would it be? I've been caring for Phoebe since she was two. About a year ago, I approached Phoebe's father and asked if, no matter what, I could be a permanent fixture in her life. He agreed, but he also said Phoebe needed the one thing he had never been able to give her: a mother. I don't know where he found you," he pointed his finger at Vicki, "but evidently, you were Plan B."

"How *did* he find you, Vicki?" I asked.

"I told you once, Phoebe, and you didn't believe me. He put an ad in the classifieds."

"A personal ad?"

"I've got it with me. I keep it with me always. I'll show you." Vicki dug into her purse for her wallet and pulled out a clipping. I held it up so Henry could read it, too:

WANTED: GROWN-UP ORPHAN
Duties include child care, elderly care. Must be kind, savvy, and want to genuinely do good in this world. Contact Ms. Ferry at 555-1273

"My father wrote this?" I could hardly believe it.

"Yes, he wanted to make sure you would be all right. He trusted the other trustee, but he wanted the legal tie, too. At first he wanted to adopt me, but we decided it would be easier and quicker just to tie the knot. Plus, it was pretty easily untied if I didn't work out. I told Bert I didn't want to be the kind of person, you know, you stick your finger in the water, and then when you pull it out, you're gone without a ripple, totally disappeared, like you never did anything, never even existed. I could certainly make a bigger splash with his fortune."

"Why an orphan?" Henry wondered out loud. "Why was that important?"

"I can guess," I said. "He wanted someone who could understand—who could know—what my life would be like." My eyes were watering, but my grin stretched all the way up to my ears. Poppy had known what was best for me, after all.

Henry hugged me again. "C'mon, what do you say we get some food? You would not believe the cuisine you can get here at the fair. You want some piggly wiggly fries perhaps, a corn dog, roasted corn on the cob, maybe even chili beans?"

"I hate beans!" I said decidedly.

Vicki patted my arm. "I'm with you, kid. That kind with the little sliced-up hot dogs? In the baked beans? That's the only kind I like."

Later, while Vicki waited in the long line for the Ladies', I turned to Henry. "What do you think Vicki is, Henry?"

"What do I think Vicki is?" he repeated, not following.

Maybe I should have challenged Henry to come up with a crossword hint for Vicki, because right at that moment, he did look kind of clueless. Patiently, I explained. "In the missing link game, Henry. Personally, I think Jimmy Wells evolved from a gnat, and not very far. But what about Vicki? What do you think she evolved from? I've been thinking about her a lot and I have a hard time with her."

"I think Vicki *is* the missing link, Phoebe. I don't think there's anyone else like her." And that's all I got out of him.

But it was enough.

12. Money Can Buy Happiness—Just Not Your Own

The sun was shining in Chicago. I helped Henry pull open the heavy brocade drapes. Sneezing from the dust, we took turns blessing each other. Sunlight spilled into the red parlor, settling into my bones like happiness, reminding me of Arizona.

The doorbell rang. I heard Vicki's voice calling from the entrance hall, "I'll get it, Henry."

Soon Vicki appeared with a pizza box and set it on the low table. I zipped off to the kitchen for napkins and plates. We sat cross-legged on the Oriental rug around the table.

"This is goooooooood pizza," I said. "I take back all the bugs. I take back all the spiders. I take back all the mean things I did to try to make you leave. I—"

"That's enough, Phoebe. I won't leave you. I made a promise to your father, but now I make that same promise to you," Vicki told me. "That is, if you can put up with me—and Auntie Ed, of course—I know I can put up with you."

"That is not a problem," I told her. "You may have noticed I'm kind of low on relatives."

"Henry?" Vicki asked.

"It is good pizza," said Henry. He had sauce on his chin, and I knew that Vicki knew he was teasing.

"Yeah, and it's free, too, Mr. Fussbudget," she told him, but she smiled when she said it.

"How did you manage that?" Henry asked. He smiled back, taking no offense.

"Abracadabra, pepperoni! Inoreppep, abracadabra!" Vicki waved her hands mysteriously forward and backward. "No, they've got a special on, just for me. Buy twelve for the homeless shelters and get one free, delivery included. We've got a *lot* of free pizza coming."

"I vote we have pizza every Friday night," I said.

"Second that," said Henry. All three of us chewed contentedly for a minute.

Then Vicki's eyes got that look in them, like she was thinking.

My eyes met Henry's. Uh oh. What now?

"You know, Phoebe," said Vicki, "the problem is you've got way too much money."

"Enough for thousands of people," I said. "I know. I could have been goat-napped!"

"It makes you a target," said Henry. "It would be different if you were an adult. It goes against my principles, but I kind of agree with Vicki."

Vicki looked flabbergasted. "You do? This has got to be a Kodak moment. Where did that camera hide? You really do, Henry?"

"I do," Henry agreed, looking straight into her eyes.

Interestingly, Vicki blushed at this. Wanting to spare my stepmother further embarrassment, I jumped in.

"When I'm grown up can I give it all away?" I asked. "Like Brooke Astor? Only I wouldn't wait until I'm that old. I could, couldn't I?"

Henry deliberated. "It's not something to do on the spur of the moment." He looked meaningfully at Vicki.

"And couldn't I give some of it away, now? I asked. "Why do I have to wait?

"You can't possibly spend it all," agreed Vicki, "but you're not old enough to make that decision."

"And Mr. Grossbeak won't like it," Henry said, "giving it away."

"Not all of it, but couldn't I give a little, Henry? In an extremely fiscally responsible way?" I asked. "All the Fortune 500 companies give money to charity. Wouldn't that be all right?"

"Maybe she could, Henry," Vicki said. "I mean, so Mr. Grossbeak won't have as many flippin' beans to count! Who cares?"

"Please, Henry, it would be one trust—whatever that word is they call me—trustling? And two trustees. Anyway, three against one." I saluted them both with a pizza slice.

Henry did the eyebrow thing again. Vicki copied him, but he was looking at me and didn't see her.

"I want to, Henry. Really I do. Only it's got to be people who really need help, people I care about."

Henry said cautiously, "If you truly want to, Phoebe, and Mr. Grossbeak agrees, I think we could look into giving some of the profits of the processing plants to charity."

"Starting with Vicki's ten million dollars, for practice," I said, laughing. "After all, she did give it back to me, Henry."

Vicki smiled back. "I did, didn't I? You go, girl. I knew you wouldn't want to be the Bean King's Daughter all your life."

She looked like she was expecting me to say something, but I didn't, not right away. I knew I would always be Albert Marchant's daughter. Poppy was a part of me; that couldn't be denied. But, maybe, just maybe, I could hold onto the part of Poppy that was the part of me to be proud of—not the bean part, amassing a fortune like a game he had to win at any cost. That had been so much of his life, but it really wasn't mine. I had thought of my father as being smart about money, stupid about love.

I looked at the woman sitting across from me, that basic save-the-world-type blonde, Vicki who dotted her *i*'s with two crazy little hearts. And beside her, Henry. Perhaps he was a little less starched now, but he remained the same man who had always been there, who would always be there, for me. I love them both, I thought. I do, too. I'm finally what they write on the cover of magazines: THE GIRL WHO HAS EVERYTHING.

Not some poor little orphan in a book. "I'll be me, myself, Phoebe."

Vicki hugged me, and Henry came up to join in from behind, so that we made a sandwich. The peanut butter got a little squished, but then, those are the best kind.